SHOULD ABORTION RIGHTS BE RESTRICTED?

Other books in the At Issue series:

Alcohol Abuse
Animal Experimentation
Anorexia
The Attack on America: September 11, 2001
Biological and Chemical Weapons
Bulimia
The Central Intelligence Agency
Cloning
Creationism vs. Evolution
Does Capital Punishment Deter Crime?
Drugs and Sports
Drunk Driving
The Ethics of Abortion
The Ethics of Genetic Engineering
The Ethics of Human Cloning
Heroin
Home Schooling
How Can Gun Violence Be Reduced?
How Should Prisons Treat Inmates?
Human Embryo Experimentation
Is Global Warming a Threat?
Islamic Fundamentalism
Is Media Violence a Problem?
Legalizing Drugs
Missile Defense
National Security
Nuclear and Toxic Waste
Nuclear Security
Organ Transplants
Performance-Enhancing Drugs
Physician-Assisted Suicide
Police Corruption
Professional Wrestling
Rain Forests
Satanism
School Shootings
Should There Be Limits to Free Speech?
Teen Sex
Video Games
What Encourages Gang Behavior?
What Is a Hate Crime?
White Supremacy Groups

SHOULD ABORTION RIGHTS BE RESTRICTED?

Auriana Ojeda, *Book Editor*

Daniel Leone, *President*
Bonnie Szumski, *Publisher*
Scott Barbour, *Managing Editor*

GREENHAVEN
PRESS ®

San Diego • Detroit • New York • San Francisco • Cleveland
New Haven, Conn. • Waterville, Maine • London • Munich

THOMSON

GALE

For more information, contact
Greenhaven Press
27500 Drake Rd.
Farmington Hills, MI 48331-3535
Or you can visit our Internet site at http://www.gale.com

LIBRARY OF CONGRESS CATALOGING-IN-PUBLICATION DATA

Should abortion rights be restricted? / Auriana Ojeda, book editor.
    p. cm. — (At issue)
Includes bibliographical references and index.
    ISBN 0-7377-1327-5 (pbk. : alk. paper) — ISBN 0-7377-1326-7 (cloth : alk. paper)
    1. Abortion—Moral and ethical aspects—United States. 2. Abortion—United States. I. Ojeda, Auriana, 1977– . II. At issue (San Diego, Calif.)
HQ767.15 .S498 2003
179.76'0973—dc21
                                             2002072224

Printed in the United States of America

Contents

Introduction

Abortion is one of the most controversial issues in American society and politics today. Since 1973, when the Supreme Court legalized abortion in its landmark *Roe v. Wade* decision, opposing groups have sought to increase or restrict access to abortion, leading to intense debates among political leaders and activists, state and federal governments, and religious organizations.

The abortion debate is often considered a two-sided controversy, but it is actually a multifaceted issue that involves questions about biology, morality, and legal rights. For example, people who consider themselves pro-life argue that abortion destroys human life, which they believe begins at conception. Therefore, abortion is immoral and should be illegal. Some pro-life advocates allow exceptions in the case of rape, incest, or when the mother's health is at risk. People who identify themselves as pro-choice contend that a woman's right to make decisions concerning her body and her future outweigh the rights of the fetus. Some pro-choice supporters endorse restrictions on abortion, such as informed consent laws, which require that a woman receive state-authored literature on abortion before undergoing the procedure, and mandatory waiting periods. One of the most controversial restrictions on abortion requires minors to notify or obtain the consent of at least one parent before having an abortion.

In 1976, a landmark Supreme Court case, *Bellotti v. Baird*, challenged a Massachusetts statute that required a minor to obtain parental consent before undergoing an abortion. The existing statute afforded a young woman the right to petition the courts if her parents refused to consent to the procedure. In addition, the statute required the courts to notify the minor's parents if she filed a bypass petition. The Supreme Court decided that the law requiring parental consent was constitutional, but, as stated by the Court, "every pregnant minor is entitled in the first instance to go directly to court for a judicial determination without prior parental notice, consultation or consent." The Court also held that minors have the right to confidentiality, and courts thereafter were prohibited from notifying a young woman's parents if she petitioned for judicial bypass.

Other provisions regulating parental consent and notification laws that *Bellotti v. Baird* set down included the requirement that a pregnant teen be given the opportunity to prove that she is mature enough to make the abortion decision on her own. If she proves that she is mature enough, the court must bypass the parental involvement requirement, a process known as judicial bypass. If the court decides that she is not mature enough, the minor must be given the opportunity to show that abortion is in her best interest. If she makes this showing, the court must grant her request. Finally, according to the court decision, the hearing must "be completed with anonymity and sufficient expedition to provide an effective opportunity for an abortion to be obtained." Thus, the courts must ensure that the judicial system does not needlessly delay the minor's abortion, which increases the costs and risks of the procedure. Subsequent court cases have upheld the standards that *Bellotti* dictated, including the controversial 1992 case *Planned Parenthood v. Casey*.

Planned Parenthood v. Casey challenged Pennsylvania's 1989 Abortion Control Act, which, among other ordinances, required a minor to obtain a parent's consent before having an abortion. The Supreme Court affirmed the *Bellotti* decision, that the parental consent law with judicial bypass was constitutional, and decided that the state may impose restrictions on abortion as long as the restrictions do not impose an "undue burden" on a woman's right to procure an abortion. Thus, according to the Court, a parental involvement law with a judicial bypass option does not unduly burden a minor seeking an abortion. The *Casey* decision validated state laws that require parental consent in a minor's abortion decision and inspired many states to enact some form of a parental involvement requirement.

According to Planned Parenthood, as of 2001, seventeen states require a minor to obtain the consent of one or both of her parents for an abortion, and fifteen states require a minor to notify one or both of her parents of her decision to have an abortion. All states with parental involvement laws provide a judicial bypass option, and some states allow grandparents, siblings, aunts, or uncles who are at least twenty-five years old to consent for the minor in place of her parent. These laws have generated intense debate among abortion activists and politicians over whether such restrictions constitute an "undue burden" on a young woman's right to seek an abortion.

Many people who are in favor of parental notification and consent laws argue that parental knowledge in a time of crisis is in the best interest of the child because parents are in the best position to protect their daughters from the risks and consequences of abortion. Supporters maintain that parents are responsible for the medical and psychological well-being of their daughters, and therefore they should be informed of any medical procedure that is performed on them. Moreover, supporters point out that parents have the right to know about other activities that their underage teens engage in that are much less significant than abortion. As stated by former democratic senatorial candidate John Pinkerton, "Parents must give consent before their child can have their ears pierced or a tattoo put on. In fact, in public schools and emergency rooms, parents must give consent before their child can be treated with so much as an aspirin. Most voters agree that it is outrageous to allow a child to undergo any surgical procedure, let alone an invasive, irreversible procedure such as an abortion, without parental notification."

Advocates of parental notification and consent laws maintain that teenagers need the support of their parents when they make a decision as potentially life-altering as abortion. These people argue that teenagers should consult their parents before they decide to have an abortion because their parents can offer experience and maturity that the teenager lacks. In addition, parental involvement laws foster communication and family unity at a time when a minor most needs the comfort of her family. According to research published in the *Journal of Adolescent Health*,

"There is little evidence . . . to suggest that parental notification legislation does harm to a teenager or her family. If anything, such requirements might support family communication and facilitate decision-making."

However, opponents of parental involvement laws argue that state laws requiring parental consent or notification are unnecessary and pose risks to pregnant teenagers. These critics contend that loving and communicative families do not need laws to foster unity, and most young women who seek abortions discuss the procedure with at least one parent anyway. A study conducted by Planned Parenthood found that 61 percent of minors who had abortions discussed their plans with at least one parent before undergoing the procedure. Of those minors who did not inform their parents of their abortions, 30 percent had histories of violence in their families, feared the occurrence of violence, or were afraid of being kicked out of their homes. The American Association of University Women states, "While the intent of such laws is to enhance family communication, the failure to guarantee confidentiality often deters young people from seeking timely services and care resulting in increased instances of sexually transmitted diseases, unwanted pregnancies, and late-term abortions."

Opponents of parental consent and notification laws, including most medical associations, allege that the judicial system causes dangerous delays for minors who seek abortions. Teenagers are more likely than older women to have later abortions anyway; court delays can prohibit a young woman from obtaining an abortion until well into the second trimester of pregnancy, increasing the risks and costs of the procedure. For example, the proportion of second trimester abortions among minors in Missouri increased by 17 percent following the enactment of a parental consent law. According to the American Academy of Pediatrics, "Legislation mandating parental involvement does not achieve the intended benefit of promoting family communication, but it does increase the risk of harm to the adolescent by delaying access to appropriate medical care. . . . [M]inors should not be compelled or required to involve their parents in their decisions to obtain abortions, although they should be encouraged to discuss their pregnancies with their parents and other responsible adults."

The argument over whether minors must involve their parents in abortion decisions is one aspect of the abortion rights controversy. *At Issue: Should Abortion Rights Be Restricted?* gives readers a thorough understanding of the legal issues surrounding the abortion debate.

1

Abortion Should Be Restricted

Michael W. McConnell

Michael W. McConnell is a professor of constitutional law at the University of Utah.

The Supreme Court's decision to legalize abortion in 1973 is not based on constitutional law. The Court alleges that the right to abortion falls under a constitutionally protected right of privacy, but no such right is mentioned in the Constitution. Moreover, the Court states that it cannot determine when life begins but implicitly denies that the fetus is a person by refusing to protect its life. Most Americans oppose abortions after the first trimester and support minor restrictions on abortion, such as parental-involvement laws and waiting periods. The Supreme Court misrepresents the will of the public by allowing women to have abortions for any reason.

On January 22, 1973, the U.S. Supreme Court handed down its decision legalizing abortion throughout the country. The day before *Roe v. Wade*, abortion was flatly illegal in almost all states, though a few had recently relaxed their laws. On the day after *Roe*, women suddenly had a constitutional right to get an abortion for any reason, a right that effectively applied at any time during the nine months of pregnancy. (In theory, states could still ban abortion in the last three months unless it was necessary for the health of the woman—but the court defined "health" so broadly as to make this limitation meaningless.) The number of abortions quickly soared to almost 1.5 million every year, roughly 30% of all pregnancies.

Roe v. Wade is the most enduringly controversial court decision of the century, and rightly so. Rather than putting the issue to rest, the court converted it into the worst sort of political struggle—one involving angry demonstrators, nasty confirmation battles and confrontational sound bites. With ordinary politicians, who are masters of compromise, out of the picture, the issue became dominated by activists of passionate intensity on both extremes of the spectrum.

Controversial decisions—even decisions that rend the body politic—are sometimes necessary. The Constitution stands for certain fundamental principles of free government, and there are times when the courts must intervene to make sure they are not neglected. But when judges act on the basis of their own political predilections, without regard to constitutional text or the decisions of representative institutions, the results are illegitimate.

The reasoning of *Roe v. Wade* is an embarrassment to those who take constitutional law seriously, even to many scholars who heartily support the outcome of the case. As John Hart Ely, former dean of Stanford Law School and a supporter of abortion rights, has written, *Roe* "is not constitutional law and gives almost no sense of an obligation to try to be."

Right of privacy

The court's reasoning proceeded in two steps. First, it found that a "right of privacy" exists under the Constitution, and that this right is "broad enough to encompass a woman's decision whether or not to terminate her pregnancy." Since this meant that the right to abortion is constitutionally protected, a state could interfere with the right only if it has a "compelling state interest" for doing so.

But the right of privacy is nowhere mentioned in the Constitution. Various judges, according to the court, had found "at least the roots of that right" in the First Amendment, in the "penumbras of the Bill of Rights," in the Ninth Amendment or in the "concept of liberty guaranteed by the first section of the Fourteenth Amendment." This vague statement is tantamount to confessing the court did not much care where in the Constitution this supposed right might be found. All that mattered was it be "broad enough" to encompass abortion.

Even assuming a right of privacy can be excavated from somewhere, anywhere, in the Constitution, what does it mean? The court avoided defining the term, except by giving examples from previous cases. The trouble is, counterexamples abound. The federal "right of privacy" has never been held to protect against laws banning drug use, assisted suicide or even consensual sodomy—just to mention a few examples of crimes that are no less "private" than abortion. It is impossible to know what does and does not fall within this nebulous category.

The right of privacy is nowhere mentioned in the Constitution.

Even assuming that there is a right of privacy, and that its contours can be discerned from the court's examples, surely it must be confined to activities that affect no one else. It would be an odd kind of privacy that confers the power to inflict injury on nonconsenting third parties. Yet the entire rationale for antiabortion laws is that an abortion does inflict injury on a nonconsenting third party, the fetus. It is not possible to describe abortion as a "privacy right" without first concluding that the fetus does not count as a third party with protectable interests.

Deciding when life begins

That brings us to step two in the court's argument. Far from resolving the thorny question of when a fetus is another person deserving of protection—surely the crux of the privacy right, if it exists—the justices determined that the issue is unresolvable. They noted that there has been a "wide divergence of thinking" regarding the "most sensitive and difficult question" of "when life begins." They stated that "[w]hen those trained in the respective disciplines of medicine, philosophy, and theology are unable to arrive at any consensus, the judiciary . . . is not in a position to speculate as to the answer."

According to the court, the existence of this uncertainty meant that the state's asserted interest in protecting unborn life could not be deemed "compelling." But this leaves us with an entirely circular argument. The supposed lack of consensus about when life begins is important because when state interests are uncertain they cannot be "compelling"; and a compelling state interest is required before the state can limit a constitutional right. But the constitutional right in question ("privacy") only exists if the activity in question does not abridge the rights of a nonconsenting third party—the very question the court says cannot be resolved. If it cannot be resolved, there is no way to determine whether abortion is a "right of privacy."

Only 15 percent [of Americans] believe that abortion should generally be available after the first three months.

In any event, the court's claim that it was not resolving the issue of "when life begins" was disingenuous. In our system, all people are entitled to protection from killing and other forms of private violence. The court can deny such protection to fetuses only if it presupposes they are not persons.

One can make a pretty convincing argument, however, that fetuses are persons. They are alive; their species is Homo sapiens. They are not simply an appendage of the mother; they have a separate and unique chromosomal structure. Surely, before beings with all the biological characteristics of humans are stripped of their rights as "persons" under the law, we are entitled to an explanation of why they fall short. For the court to say it cannot "resolve the difficult question of when life begins" is not an explanation.

It is true, of course, that people honestly disagree about the question of when life begins. But divergence of opinion is not ordinarily a reason to take a decision away from the people and their elected representatives. One of the functions of democratic government is to provide a forum for debating and ultimately resolving controversial issues. Judges cannot properly strike down the acts of the political branches that do not clearly violate the Constitution. If no one knows when life begins, the courts have no basis for saying the legislature's answer is wrong. To be sure, abortion is an explosive issue, with noisy and self-righteous advocates on both sides. But the Supreme Court made it far more so by eliminating the possibility of reasoned legislative deliberation and prudent compromise.

Public opinion

It is often said that abortion is an issue that defies agreement or compromise. But if the polling data are correct, there has been a broad and surprisingly stable consensus among the American people for at least the past 30 years that rejects the uncompromising positions of both pro-choice and pro-life advocates. Large majorities (61% in a *New York Times*/CBS poll) believe that abortion should be legally available during the early months of pregnancy. There is also widespread support for legal abortions when the reasons are sufficiently weighty (rape, incest, probability of serious birth defect, serious danger to the mother's health).

But only 15% believe that abortion should generally be available after the first three months, when the fetus has developed a beating heart, fingers and toes, brain waves and a full set of internal organs. Majorities oppose abortions for less weighty reasons, such as avoiding career interruptions. Even larger majorities (approaching 80%) favor modest regulations, like waiting periods and parental consent requirements, to guard against hasty and ill-informed decisions. (The Supreme Court has permitted some such regulations to stand in the years since *Roe*.) Most Americans would prohibit particularly grisly forms of the procedure, like partial-birth abortions.

These opinions have persisted without significant change since the early 1970s, and are shared by women and men, young and old alike. On the question of abortion, Americans overwhelmingly reject the extremes. If the courts would get out of the business of regulating abortion, most legislatures would pass laws reflecting the moderate views of the great majority. This would provide more protection than the unborn have under current law, though probably much less than pro-life advocates would wish.

The Supreme Court brought great discredit on itself by overturning state laws regulating abortion without any persuasive basis in constitutional text or logic. And to make matters worse, it committed these grave legal errors in the service of an extreme vision of abortion rights that the vast majority of Americans rightly consider unjust and immoral. *Roe v. Wade* is a useful reminder that government by the representatives of the people is often more wise, as well as more democratic, than rule by lawyers in robes.

2

Abortion Should Not Be Restricted

Diana Brown

Diana Brown is the former chairman of the London-based organization Population Concern. She also represents the International Humanist and Ethical Union at the United Nations in Geneva.

Abortion is a public health issue because if legal abortion is unavailable, women will risk injury, infection, and death from medically unsafe abortions to end an undesired pregnancy. Abortion should be legal because the rights of the mother supercede the rights of the fetus, especially because the fetus shows no sign of self-awareness until well into the second trimester. Recently, the United States has made attempts to safeguard the rights of the fetus, but this practice draws arbitrary lines that determine when the fetus is viable. If anti-choice advocates want to eliminate abortion, they should support strategies to reduce unwanted pregnancy, such as sex education and contraception.

Every year some 45 million pregnancies, out of a total of 175 million, end in abortion. Nearly half of those abortions (20 million) are medically unsafe, resulting in the deaths of nearly 80,000 women a year and a much larger number suffering infection, injury, and trauma. Thus the legality of abortion and the availability of medically safe abortion are public health issues. Criminalizing abortion does not save babies; it kills mothers.

Women have always resorted to abortion and probably always will. The difference now is that modern, safe, medical and surgical methods are available. Many countries have legalized abortion. According to the United Nations Population Fund, "Where abortion is safe and widely available, and other reproductive health services are in place, rates of abortion tend to be low. The simple conclusion is: better contraceptive services for all people will reduce abortion."

On public health grounds I am in no doubt that safe abortion should be freely available on request by the pregnant woman, at least up to some agreed time limit. The woman's reasons for wanting an abortion should not be relevant, even though many of us might not approve of them. For example, as a result of pressures caused by the low status of females in her society, a woman may well wish to practice selective abortion of female fetuses. This is not in the interests of the community as a whole, and certainly will do nothing to advance the cause of women in general. Should she nevertheless be permitted to do it, or should society prohibit it? I would come down strongly for the right of the individual woman to decide for herself. If we believe that Western women have a right to choose, then so should all women, even though their choices may be socially inconvenient. More effort should go into removing the causes of abortion than into eradicating the practice.

Because of the constant struggle first to allow and then to preserve legal abortion, attitudes have become polarized: one is either "pro-life" or "pro-choice," and anyone who falls somewhere in the middle can be blamed for comforting the enemy, so I shall no doubt be attacked for my views.

The status of the fetus

Central to the debate on abortion is the biological, legal, and moral status of the fetus. The "pro-lifers" are in no doubt that a fertilized ovum is a human being and that its destruction is murder. Some "pro-choice" supporters maintain that the fetus, far from being a human being, is merely a part of the mother's body and is entirely hers to dispose of, so that deciding to have an abortion is of no more significance than deciding to get one's hair cut. Since the fetus is, however, genetically distinct from the mother, the latter position is hard to sustain.

Traditional objections to abortion have not seen it as murder. Anglo-Saxon law has not traditionally seen the fetus as a legal person. This position has recently been reinforced in England, where a woman's right to physical autonomy and to refuse treatment (a caesarian section) just before or during birth has been recognized, even after a warning that she is risking the death of her baby. In the United States, however, there appear to be moves toward according legal rights to fetuses in certain circumstances. If these are consolidated, it has obvious implications for abortion and for the status of the pregnant woman.

> *More effort should go into removing the causes of abortion than into eradicating the practice.*

The development of life is a continuous process. Any line drawn across it for legal purposes is essentially arbitrary. Even if one takes the extreme "pro-life" position, there is no way at present of knowing exactly when or whether conception has taken place. Wherever we draw the line on the abortion scale—at 10 weeks, 18 weeks, 24 weeks, or at any moment up to natural birth—it is an arbitrary decision: you may have a legal abortion, say, at 167 days but not at 169. The law requires definite cut-off points, but the moral position is fuzzier.

If a woman has an absolute right to choose, can she abort a fetus at

39 weeks, when clearly it would be viable? If we put a time limit on abortions, there is no essential moral difference between the status of a fetus one day before the limit and one day after. If we do not put a time limit on abortions, then why choose the moment of birth as a cutoff point? Why not permit infanticide? What happens if an aborted fetus is born alive? Should it be treated as a baby, or as something to be disposed of?

Humanist morality

Rather than just attacking the arguments of religious fanatics, we should debate these issues from a humanist point of view. They are more complex than just accepting "a woman's right to choose," even though honor is due to those who have struggled to establish that principle. A woman who decides whether or not to have an abortion is making a moral decision, and we need to look at the principles involved.

Most people do not believe that abortion is outright murder, but many find it vaguely distasteful. You do not find the same problem with contraception. Why should this be? An obvious difference is that, whereas contraception prevents the initiation of new life, abortion destroys a living process that has already begun.

If anti-choice advocates are really against abortion, they should be in favor of measures that are known to reduce the incidence of abortion.

If we ignore religious ideas of souls and the sacredness of any form of human life, we may note that the early fetus, although human, is neither sentient nor capable of independent existence. It would seem therefore to deserve less consideration than a live mouse, which is both.

Legal time limits are often based on the concept of the viability of the fetus: its ability to survive ex utero. But there is no clear point at which a fetus automatically becomes viable, and it is not always easy to determine the exact stage of the pregnancy. Moreover, as medical advances change the limits, we could conceivably one day be faced with the possibility of total progression in vitro from fertilization to full-term development. This *Brave New World* scenario would mean that no aborted fetus could of necessity be discarded as nonviable.

Author Bonnie Steinbock suggests that the key concept is "interest": all and only beings who have interests have moral status. She regards sentience as a necessary condition for having interests. We may wish to protect and preserve a building, but it does not matter to the building itself whether it is pulled down or not. It is without interests, although human beings may themselves have interest in its preservation. A dog, on the other hand, does have interest in its own continued health and well-being, so we may consider it for its own sake, and not just for the sake of its owner. Even living things, for example, plants, may lack interest in this sense.

Compared with a live, sentient dog, a pre-sentient fetus, lacking any enjoyment or awareness of its "life," has not yet developed interests and can therefore be considered not to be a moral object. By about 22 weeks' gestation, when it may be capable of rudimentary pleasure or pain and possibly a kind of consciousness, it may be said to have interests and to be owed moral consideration.

This does not necessarily mean that it should be accorded the same consideration as an already-born human being, any more than we would accord the same consideration to a dog. People who talk of the rights of a fetus often seem to forget that those rights can only exist with the acquiescence of the mother. She is not just a container for a fetus; she is an undoubted full human being with rights of her own to bodily self-determination. She herself is, however, morally bound to consider the interest of her fetus as it approaches birth. While I believe that the choice should be that of only the woman, I also believe (to borrow words from the traditional Anglican marriage service) that abortion "is not by any to be enterprised . . . unadvisedly, lightly or wantonly."

Fighting "pro-life" hypocrisy

We should attack the anti-choice advocates for their lack of consistency and outright hypocrisy. In fact, they can be shown up as being not so much against abortion, or "pro-life" (whatever that means), but against sex. Unwanted pregnancy is seen as a punishment for illicit sex and abortion as a means of escaping the consequences. Anyone who can remember how single mothers and illegitimate children were treated by religious fanatics in the days before legal abortion will know that the punishment was enthusiastically prolonged by the righteous. There wasn't much of a "pro-life" stance then.

If anti-choice advocates are really against abortion, they should be in favor of measures that are known to reduce the incidence of abortion. Most of the same people who are now against legal abortion oppose full and frank sex education in schools—and yet it has been shown that good sex education can delay the start of teenage sexual experience. They also tend to oppose free access to a full range of contraceptive services and believe that religious indoctrination alone will guard against unwanted pregnancies. Humanists can point to the enlightened practices of the Netherlands, where safe, legal abortion is easily available, but everyone receives good sex education and information about contraception, and there are very good contraceptive services. The Netherlands has one of the lowest rates of abortion in the world.

Grounds for abortion

Many countries that permit legal abortion restrict the grounds on which abortion can be allowed. Some allow it when the fetus is known to be handicapped or when the health of the mother is threatened. Other countries permit abortion in cases of rape or incest but not otherwise. But surely the moral position of an unwanted fetus resulting from a crime is no different from that of any other. Either fetuses at that state of development merit legal protection or they don't.

3

Abortion Rights Devalue the Fetus

Richard Stith

Richard Stith is a professor of law at Valparaiso University. He holds a Ph.D. in religious studies as well as a law degree from Yale University.

The Supreme Court's 1973 decision, *Roe v. Wade*, legalized elective abortion until viability and abortion to protect the life of the mother after viability. The Court's decision mandates that the fetus has no inner nature until birth, which suggests that an entity's inner nature depends upon where the entity is located. In 1992, in *Planned Parenthood v. Casey*, the Supreme Court reaffirmed the legality of abortion, but also awarded moderate rights to the fetus, as reflected in mandatory waiting periods, informed consent, and parental involvement laws. However, the *Casey* decision relied primarily on the precedent set by *Roe*—that the difference between abortion and infanticide depends upon the location of the fetus. This logic denies the unborn the constitutional right to equal protection and may lead to the devaluation of other vulnerable forms of human life.

In its famous 1973 decision, *Roe v. Wade*, the United States Supreme Court mandated elective abortion up to viability, and abortion for broadly defined "health" reasons (i.e., virtually elective abortion) thereafter. That opinion contains a deep contradiction that can be understood as a conflict between what I will call "nominalism" and "realism." The Court asserts in effect that the unborn child has no real nature, that what it is is solely a matter of conventions concerning names (nomina in Latin). Yet the moment of birth is assumed to mark an essential difference, a real (not merely conventional) transition to a living entity, human in nature.

In the past twenty-five years, this "birth wall" has been largely dismantled or, to use appropriately the more fashionable expression, "deconstructed." That is, the purely nominal character of the birth difference has become increasingly accepted by those on both sides of the abortion debate. My purpose here is to elucidate this shift and to show the possibilities and perils of our emerging legal world.

Deciding when life begins

Roe's nominalism can be seen most simply in Justice Harry Blackmun's well-known assertion that the Justices "need not resolve the difficult question of when life begins" in order to justify the Court's requirement that legislators treat the fetus at most as "the potentiality of human life" right up to the moment of birth. There is no need, he says, to answer this question because the diversity of answers given by others shows the question to be unanswerable, at least at present. But surely the law may take controvertible stands, and it may seek to minimize the possible harm of error even where it has no access to truth. Blackmun's insistence that what we call the fetus does not matter seems to imply a much more radical agnosticism: the assumption that the names we give to pre-born human beings are wholly conventional, that one can in principle never say that abortion really takes a human life.

Blackmun's justificatory history of permissive abortion practices bears out this appearance of deep-seated nominalism. Let me explain. In order to decide whether or not practices of past ages can be justified today, we ought to look not only at the practices themselves (e.g., practices permitting abortion), but also at the beliefs about values and facts upon which those practices were based. If those underlying values now seem to us quite mistaken, the practices arising from those beliefs hold no authority for us today. Similarly, we cannot honestly invoke the authority of past scientific conclusions if we now see that the data upon which the conclusions were based were incomplete or mistaken. If we seek to know what is real, we cannot rest content with labels. We have to inquire into reasons.

Yet throughout Justice Blackmun's lengthy surveys of past practices allowing abortion, he never once asks whether or not the beliefs upon which those practices were based are in fact ones that he considers admirable or accurate. (By contrast, by the way, he occasionally does try to refute past reasons for restricting abortion—such as to protect the mother's life.)

The purely nominal character of the birth difference has become increasingly accepted.

For example, Blackmun refers often to "quickening" as a popular dividing line, without once mentioning that modern medical knowledge shows this "event," as he calls it, to be an illusion. The overall impression Blackmun gives is that whether and when abortion is allowed is an open choice, with most cultures voting for abortion.

At the same time, Blackmun suggests (without exactly stating) that birth makes a real difference. Such a claim is implicit in his refusal to find that constitutional personhood or actual human life begins "before live birth." In any event, Justice John Paul Stevens, writing thirteen years later in support of *Roe v. Wade*, makes clear the necessity of what I have here called "the birth wall." Concurring in *Thornburgh v. American College of Obstetricians and Gynecologists* (1986), he insists that "there is a fundamental and well-recognized difference between a fetus and a human being; indeed, if there is not such a difference, the permissibility of terminating the life of a fetus could scarcely be left to the will of the state legislatures." In the next sentence, Stevens makes clear that, in his view, even "the nine-month-gestated, fully sentient fetus on the eve of birth" is not yet a human being.

We are to presume that the unborn child or fetus has no inner nature of its own.

Stevens gives no explanation for his claim that a fundamental change at birth is required in order to justify legal abortion. But one basis for his view is surely the principle of human equality that underlies both our ethics and our law. There must be a real and deep difference between human and nonhuman entities in order to give force and limit to the normative demand for equal protection for all humans. If any and all entities could be defined at will into or out of humanity, human equality would have no practical significance. Insofar as human equality does make practical demands on us, it follows that we are politically committed to ontological realism. Stevens has to claim that a fetus and an infant are different kinds of beings in order to avoid recognizing an equal right to life before and after birth. Only if expulsion from the womb gives the fetus a human nature for the first time is late-term abortion easily justified.

The inner nature of the fetus

We are thus bequeathed a curious antinomy by *Roe*. We are to presume that the unborn child or fetus has no inner nature of its own. What it is called is a matter of convention or preference, for it is not "really" anything at all. At the same time, we must assume that birth is a bright line, a moment when (in reality not merely in convention), by leaving the uterus, the fetus becomes undeniably one of us. In other words, we are to be skeptical nominalists prior to birth, but credulous realists about birth itself.

It should be obvious, even to Stevens, that the notion of a clear, fundamental difference at birth is not, shall we say, viable. The many postmodern nominalists among us (especially among academics) can hardly be expected to accept the mere assertion that a bright line between human and nonhuman exists at birth. If definition in principle is social construction, Stevens' definition of humanity will inevitably be deconstructed by those who have the political will to do so—i.e., those interested in protecting the unborn or in justifying infanticide (of which more below).

But even realists must in the end reject the birth-wall thesis, because it claims that what something is depends upon where it is. It makes the fundamental nature of the perinatal entity depend solely upon location. But location cannot determine a being's inner nature, though location may well affect how that being functions for others and thus affect what they name it. That is, the jurisprudence of Blackmun and Stevens abjures the search for the nature of the fetus prior to birth, where a realist would search it out, while relying on a form of naive realism about birth itself, where the fetus/infant difference cannot be more than nominal. Blackmun and Stevens would have us believe the child born prematurely at seven months to be a human being, while its more developed cousin in the womb overdue at nine and a half months is still a creature without a fundamentally human nature. Without an appeal to some supernatural change such as the insertion of a soul at first breath, an appeal which neither judge makes nor constitutionally could make, such a belief is quite simply absurd, beyond the limits of even the most extreme credulity.

The absurdity of the birth wall has not caused it to fall entirely. The Supreme Court in fact reaffirmed *Roe v. Wade* in 1992 in *Planned Parenthood v. Casey*, but it did so without claiming that birth really makes a difference, explicitly avoiding any claim that Roe was rightly decided in the first place. Instead, *Casey* based the right to abort in large measure on stare decisis, binding precedent, which is in *Casey* a doctrine of court vanity and positivism. Past decisions cannot be overturned just because they were based on fallacious reasoning. Fidelity to the Constitution is not by itself a sufficient reason to right old wrongs. Only on the basis of new information not available to the earlier Court can erroneous holdings be overruled. Except in such circumstances, to correct past mistakes would undermine the Supreme Court's prestige, *Casey* argued, particularly so on matters of great controversy. The abortion flat stands, but only as such. Not willing to deny (or even explicitly to consider) that millions of actual human lives are being lost under *Roe, Casey* says simply that the Court has spoken, causa finita est.

There is no real difference between abortion and infanticide.

Referring to "the interest of the State in the protection of 'potential life,'" also characterized as "a legitimate interest in promoting the life or potential life of the unborn," the outcome-determinative opinion of Justices Sandra Day O'Connor, Anthony Kennedy, and David Souter declared in sum:

> We do not need to say whether each of us, had we been members of the Court when the valuation of the state interest came before it as an original matter, would have concluded, as the Roe Court did, that its weight is insufficient to justify a ban on abortions prior to viability even when it is subject to certain exceptions. The matter is not before us in the first instance, and coming as it does after nearly twenty years of litigation in Roe's wake we are satisfied that the immediate question is not the soundness of Roe's resolution of the issue, but the precedential force that must be accorded to its holding.

There is good news and bad news in *Casey's* doubts about *Roe*. The good news is that, since the Court no longer assumes that a magical change comes about at birth, the unchanging identity of the child before and after birth can be affirmed in law—provided always that the ultimate right to abortion be preserved. Postnatal realism can begin to replace prenatal nominalism. If the child has real dignity outside the womb, it must have dignity inside—since location cannot make an essential difference. Again in the words of O'Connor, Kennedy, and Souter: "Regulations which do no more than create a structural mechanism by which the State . . . may express profound respect for the life of the unborn are permitted, if they are not a substantial obstacle to the woman's exercise of the right to choose." For example, laws requiring a woman contemplating abortion to be fully informed about the procedure, including what it does to the fetus, were declared constitutional by *Casey* (overruling a contrary 1983 holding that had read *Roe* to forbid state attempts to dissuade women from having abortions).

If unequal treatment of human beings is acceptable, the need to assert a fundamental difference between fetus and infant disappears.

Even in the earliest stages of pregnancy, a state may enact rules and regulations designed to encourage women to know that there are philosophic and social arguments of great weight that can be brought to bear in favor of continuing the pregnancy to full term: "Measures aimed at ensuring that a woman's choice contemplates the consequences for the fetus do not necessarily interfere with the right recognized in *Roe*."

Though it sometimes still uses the opaque and demeaning phrase "potential life" (along with "life" and "child") for the living human fetus, the *Casey* decision clearly permits state anti-abortion laws to be motivated by the "legitimate goal of protecting the life of the unborn," so long as their purpose remains "to persuade the woman to choose childbirth" rather than forcibly to stop her from choosing abortion. Indeed, already in the 1989 *Webster* case, the birth distinction had weakened to the point where the Court upheld Missouri legislation requiring that the unborn child, from the moment of conception, be treated as a legal person except insofar as the decisions of the U.S. Supreme Court might otherwise require.

In addition to informed consent, *Casey* approves a twenty-four-hour period of reflection between the time the pregnant woman is given the required information and the actual abortion. But *Casey's* persuade-but-do-not-actually-block principle need not stop there. After that case was decided, for example, Pennsylvania initiated a system of state subsidies for (nonreligious, of course) pro-life crisis pregnancy centers, the sort that had previously subsisted almost solely on private contributions and volunteers. And if women already in a crisis pregnancy can be given accurate factual information intended to encourage them to choose life, why not public high school students, even as part of a required curriculum? Such information may well be more effectively integrated into decision-making if it is provided prior to a pregnancy-induced sense of desperation. Just such an educational initiative appears to be beginning in Florida.

Where the Court-declared constitutional right to abortion is not even peripherally at issue, the Supreme Court has been still more indulgent regarding state action designed to protect unborn human beings. Just recently, for example, it refused to review the South Carolina Supreme Court's decision upholding a statute punishing drug use by pregnant women as a form of "child endangerment." And at no point post-*Roe* has the U.S. Supreme Court ever struck down any of the laws, now found in the majority of states, that punish the killing of a fetus whenever the killing is done without the mother's permission. In Minnesota today, an assailant who intentionally destroys a just-conceived human embryo—by battering its mother, for example—can be sentenced to life in prison for "murder of an unborn child," even if the woman was on her way to an abortion clinic at the time.

The benefits of the *Casey* decision

The good news, then, is that *Roe*'s never-absolute birth wall was partially dismantled by the *Casey* decision, permitting greater recognition and protection for the child prior to birth. *Roe*'s postnatal realism has begun, to a degree, to displace its prenatal nominalism.

The "bad news" is of a piece with the good: The weakness of the birth wall, the absurdity of thinking that a child's location (or its mother's choice) can change its inner nature, can easily permit *Roe*'s pre-birth nominalism to expand to displace realism after birth as well. For someone committed to *Roe*, the realization that there is no real difference between abortion and infanticide can mean only that infanticide must, at least in principle, be permitted.

This logic can be seen at work in the current widespread support among pro-choice advocates for the right to kill a fetus during induced delivery. If the child partially outside the womb could be protected against having its brain sucked out, how could exactly the same child still wholly inside be dismembered with impunity? In order to avoid this question, the right to partial-birth abortion must be affirmed with vigor.

But even clearer, I think, has been the apparently universal support for infanticide in pro-abortion scholarship. I am thinking here of the works of people like Joseph Fletcher, Michael Tooley, Ronald M. Green, Jonathan Glover, Peter Singer, and perhaps Steven Pinker, but to my knowledge they represent not just a majority, but a very solid consensus. A survey by Don Marquis in the *Journal of Philosophy* showed that all pro-choice theories developed by 1989 deny that there is anything wrong prima facie with killing infants. I know of no pro-abortion scholar who has written that there is something intrinsically wrong with early postnatal infanticide. The reason is obvious: if the newborn has intrinsic (real, in our terms) dignity, then the same child located in the womb just prior to birth must have equal dignity. Indeed, if the newborn infant has inherent dignity, even the just-conceived embryo must have a like dignity, for the only humanly significant attributes possessed by the newborn are possessed as well by the embryo: membership in our species and (what comes to the same thing) design for human community, with its virtues of reason and love.

To say that actual manifestation of (rather than mere design for) these virtues is required for human dignity would be to exclude the infant along with the embryo. To focus upon the actualized traits possessed by the infant but not the embryo (e.g., size or ability to survive with less external life support) would be to include many nonhuman entities and, moreover, would be to point to traits that are ultimately just not very important to our idea of human dignity. For this very reason, the German Constitutional Court ruled unanimously in 1975, with an entirely different panel reaffirming also unanimously in 1993, that the constitutional right to life must extend throughout pregnancy. Since we know that newborn infants have human dignity, despite the fact that their uniquely human virtues subsist only as potentialities, we cannot deny that same dignity to the unborn, who possess those same potentialities. In the words of the German court:

> The process of development . . . is a continuing process which exhibits no sharp demarcation and does not allow a precise division of the various steps of development of the human life. The process does not end with birth; the phenomena of consciousness which are specific to the human personality, for example, appear for the first time a rather long time after birth. Therefore, the protection . . . of the Basic Law cannot be limited either to the "completed" human being after birth or to the child about to be born which is independently capable of living. . . . [N]o distinction can be made here between various stages of the life developing itself before birth, or between unborn and born life.

Many pro-abortion academics do claim to discern a bright line at a later, post-infantile stage of human life. For example, H. Tristam Engelhardt, Jr. has averred that true personhood inheres only in the normal adult human. Such thinkers are still realists; they just think that what really matters begins quite a bit later than birth. And, in their favor, it must be admitted that almost any developmental point they might choose—e.g., self-consciousness, the age of reason, even puberty—will be more real and thus more arguable than *Roe's* choice of birth. But can such points remain bright lines in the postmodern era? If the existence of the self is a cognitive illusion, as some argue, how can self-consciousness really matter? If reason is only manipulation, an epiphenomenon of the will to power, why should it matter more than, say, muscles? It is vain to suppose that new attempts to construct real walls against killing can be successful in our age of deconstruction.

Human equality

Rather than search vainly for a new bright line after birth, more perspicacious pro-abortion jurists have opted to rid themselves of the principle to which we pointed early in this essay, a principle that makes it necessary to have bright lines in the first place: human equality. If human beings can be treated in radically unequal ways, if they need not even in principle be accorded equal protection under the law, then those who favor abortion need not be disturbed by the continuity of human life. If unequal treatment of human beings is acceptable, the need to assert a fundamental difference between fetus and infant disappears. Why bother wracking one's brain to find a difference if they need not be shown equal respect, even granting their common humanity?

Among academics, Ronald Dworkin has perhaps done the most to advance human inequality in the law. "The less profitable effort invested in each human being, the less regrettable the killing of that being" paraphrases a non-egalitarian notion that Dworkin applies throughout the human life span, after as well as before birth.

We can begin to treat the pre-born with respect equal to that which we now show to already-born human beings.

But some of our federal appellate judges (not yet with explicit U.S. Supreme Court approval) have cut even more directly to the quick. Seeking to justify lesser state protection for the lives of those terminally disabled, in 1996 Judge Roger Miner wrote for the Second Circuit, "Surely the state's interest lessens as the potential for life diminishes." For the Ninth Circuit in the same year, Judge Stephen Reinhardt wrote: "[The strength of] the state's interest in preserving life . . . is dependent on relevant circumstances, including the medical condition . . . of the person whose life is at stake." Judge Robert Beezer, writing in dissent, countered that the court is thus reexamining "the historic presumption that all human lives are equally and intrinsically valuable," and that this reexamination may be "a mere rationalization for house-cleaning, cost-cutting, and burden-shifting—a way to get rid of those whose lives we deem worthless."

Perhaps because of Judge Beezer's forceful challenge, Judge Reinhardt sought to bolster his position with the Supreme Court's jurisprudence denying equal protection to the unborn:

> In right-to-die cases, the outcome of the balancing test may differ at different points along the life cycle as a person's physical or medical condition deteriorates, just as in abortion cases the permissibility of restrictive state legislation may vary with the progression of the pregnancy. . . . [B]oth types of cases raise issues of life and death.

Judge Beezer did not attempt to deny the majority's analogy to abortion law, just to narrow it:

> [I]n the abortion context, the Supreme Court tells us that the state's interests in fetal life are weaker before viability than they are once the fetus becomes viable. . . . A state's interest in preserving human life is stronger when applied to viable beings than it is when applied to nonviable beings. Like a first-trimester fetus, a person kept alive by life-sustaining treatment is essentially nonviable. A terminally ill patient seeking to commit physician-assisted suicide, by contrast, is essentially viable. The patient may be inexorably approaching the line of nonviability. But the patient is still

on the viable side of that line, and consequently enjoys the full protection of the state's interest in preserving life.

Of course, since even fully viable fetuses enjoy nowhere near the "full protection" of the Constitution under *Roe* and *Casey*, Judge Beezer's analogy is cold comfort even for the disabled person capable of surviving without life supports. If such a person counts only as much as a viable fetus, he will get far less than equal protection from our law.

In denying the constitutional duty of equal protection, are these appellate judges doing anything more than following the lead of *Casey*? In holding that *Roe* must stand even if it was wrongly decided, *Casey* proclaimed that the State's duty of equal protection falls before stare decisis and the prestige needs of the Court. Reinhardt and Beezer read that case well.

The honesty newly permitted by the *Casey* decision thus cuts in two directions. The fact that the same child exists within and without the womb can lead us to two opposite conclusions. We can begin to treat the pre-born with respect equal to that which we now show to already-born human beings. Or we can come to treat some of those already born with the same disrespect we now show toward the pre-born. We can become more realistic about the entire human life span, or we can begin to doubt the human nature of others thought inconvenient and less capable. Or we may finesse the whole problem of nominalism vs. realism by denying the State's duty of equal protection, leaving the weak to their own devices regardless of whether they are human in nature or only in name.

4

Partial-Birth Abortion Is Legal Infanticide

Brian Fahling

Brian Fahling is the senior trial attorney for the American Family Association's Center for Law and Policy.

In June 2000, the Supreme Court declared in *Stenberg v. Carhart* that a Nebraska statute that forbade partial-birth abortion was unconstitutional. Nebraska's statute was based upon the medical and legal definition of abortion, which defines abortion as the death of the fetus within the uterus. The partial-birth abortion procedure requires induced labor and the partial delivery of the fetus before it is killed. Once the fetus passes through the cervix and into the vaginal canal, the birth process has begun, and the term "abortion" no longer applies. The 1973 Supreme Court ruling, *Roe v. Wade*, guaranteed a woman's right to choose abortion, but it did not grant her the right to kill an infant who is in the process of being born. The partial-birth abortion procedure is tantamount to legal infanticide.

Rutgers College of Law professor Sherry Colb, in her April 2000 article, "What The Frozen Embryo Cases Can Teach Us About The "Partial-Birth" Abortion Case," tells us a good deal more about the twisted logic of persecution than frozen embryos. Professor Colb is clearly worried that the Supreme Court has no basis in its existing jurisprudence to strike Nebraska's partial-birth "abortion" statute if it should get beyond the technical challenges and into the merits of the case. And she has good reason to be worried because application of the Court's jurisprudence to the Nebraska statute would undoubtedly result in it being found constitutional. Professor Colb thinks this would be a bad result, I would applaud it. But before considering the professor's Hitlerian rationale for perpetuating the practice of killing "nonviable" infants in the process of being born, it is necessary to explain the argument in favor of partial-birth "abortion" bans that she attempts to overcome in her article.

Misleading terminology

It is unfortunate that the procedure that is regulated by Nebraska's statute is described as partial-birth "abortion" because it is misleading. It is misleading because, medically speaking, one cannot abort a living fetus that is partially vaginally delivered. This is so because, according to *Dorlands Illustrated Medical Dictionary*, abortion is "the premature expulsion from the uterus of the products of conception," and vaginal delivery is "delivery of an infant through the normal openings of the uterus and vagina [partial vaginal delivery would, then, be the partial delivery of an infant. . .]."

In other words, an abortion always contemplates intrauterine fetal death which is by force of logical and medical necessity exclusive of death that is purposely achieved extrauterine, that is, delivery of the child or infant into the vaginal canal (or beyond) where it is then killed. So, it is clear that in regulating partial-birth "abortion," Nebraska is not regulating abortion at all as that term is medically and legally understood, but rather, is merely proscribing the killing of an infant that has been delivered from the uterus into the vaginal canal.

The passage of the infant from the uterus into the vaginal canal signals a momentous medical, and now legal, event. Thus, Nebraska's statute has given effect to the medical distinction between the locus where intrauterine fetal stasis is maintained (and where abortions take place) and the dynamic irreversible process of birth which begins when the membranes are ruptured and the fetus emerges through the cervical os into the vaginal canal, concluding with the complete separation of the infant from the mother. By its terms, then, the statute regulates the process of birth, also referred to as parturition, which commences when the living fetus begins to exit the womb. Birth begins, and complete birth is inevitable, once the membrane of the amniotic sac is punctured and the fetus begins its emergence from the womb through the cervical os.

The passage of an infant from the uterus into the vaginal canal signals a momentous medical, and now legal, event.

Because the statute does not regulate abortion, cases such as *Roe v. Wade* (1973) and *Planned Parenthood of S.E. Pennsylvania v. Casey* (1992) are inapposite. Nevertheless, these cases highlight the fact it is birth, and not abortion, that is being regulated by the statute. *Roe* and its progeny all speak in terms of the "unborn" child, that is, fetuses who are not in the process of being born. As the Court in *Roe* observed, "[the pregnant woman] carries an embryo and, later, a fetus, if one accepts the medical definition of the developing young in the human uterus." The Court did in fact accept the medical definitions in crafting its opinion in *Roe*, and it only seems reasonable to expect that it will do so again in considering Nebraska's statute.

It is beyond dispute that the Supreme Court has always understood abortion to mean the intrauterine killing of a fetus. Indeed, the partial delivery of a living infant with the express purpose of killing it is a recent innovation by abortion doctors and could not have been foreseen by the Supreme Court in its abortion jurisprudence, predicated as it is, on medical definitions that themselves comprehend only intrauterine death, and a history of abortion, particularly as exhaustively recounted in *Roe*, wherein not even a hint of the procedure proscribed by Nebraska's statute can be found.

Moreover, unlike the *Roe* Court which was unwilling to accept Texas' invitation to "resolve the difficult question of when life begins," because "the judiciary, at this point in the development of man's knowledge, is not in position to speculate as to the answer," there is, here, no need for us to speculate about when birth begins. There is no raging debate or lack of consensus about the process of birth among "those trained in the respective disciplines of medicine, philosophy, and theology." Birth, as shown above, is an irreversible process that will result in the complete delivery of the infant whether viable or non-viable. Even the non-viable fetus who is prematurely and artificially pulled from the womb, past the cervical os and into the vaginal canal, will be born alive if not killed by a doctor during the birth process.

Right to choose

Since *Roe*, there has been a recognized constitutional right to choose to terminate a pregnancy, there is, however, no corresponding constitutional right to kill, or to choose to kill, an infant who is in the process of being born. The substantive due process analysis that birthed, so to speak, the right to abortion, is not now constitutionally pregnant with a fundamental right to kill a partially born infant. This common sense conclusion is confirmed through application of the analytical framework established by the Supreme Court to locate substantive due process rights. The structure of the Court's substantive due process framework consists of two primary features. The first feature considers whether the right claimed or liberty interest asserted is "objectively, deeply rooted in this Nation's history and tradition."

Stated in different terms, is the right or liberty interest asserted "so rooted in the traditions and conscience of our people as to be ranked as fundamental, and implicit in the concept of ordered liberty, such that neither liberty nor justice would exist if they were sacrificed. . . ." The second feature considered by the Court is the requirement of "a careful description of the asserted fundamental liberty interest."

There is . . . no . . . constitutional right to kill, or to choose to kill, an infant who is in the process of being born.

There is no evidence, either in *Roe* or its progeny, that a right to kill, or to choose to kill, an infant that has been partially vaginally delivered is "objectively, deeply rooted in this Nation's history and tradition." As the Court has stated, "[o]ur Nation's history, legal traditions, and practices provide the crucial guideposts for responsible decision making, that direct and restrain our exposition of the Due Process Clause." The second feature of the analysis requires a "careful" description of the asserted fundamental liberty interest, to wit: whether the "liberty" specially protected by the Due Process Clause includes a right to kill, or to choose to kill, an infant that has been partially vaginally delivered? Therefore, one may conclude that the Due Process Clause is not so elastic that it may be stretched to include such a right.

If partial-birth abortion is protected as a constitutional right, it is likely . . . to yield a much broader license.

The Supreme Court, then, requires that Nebraska's ban on partial-birth abortions be rationally related to legitimate government interests. This requirement is unquestionably met by the state's regulation. Nebraska fears that permitting partial-birth abortions will start it down the path to infanticide. If partial-birth abortion is protected as a constitutional right, it is likely, in effect, to yield a much broader license, which could prove extremely difficult to police and contain. For example, if a doctor may kill an infant who has passed one-fifth into the birth canal, why may he not kill the infant who has passed four-fifths into the birth canal?; and if he may kill the infant who has passed four-fifths into the birth canal, why may he not kill the infant who is completely separated from her mother? So, Nebraska's interest in erecting an impenetrable barrier against infanticide presents a compelling slippery slope argument quite similar to that embraced by the Court in *Washington v. Glucksberg* (1997). In *Glucksberg,* the Court recognized "that what is couched as a limited right to 'physician-assisted suicide' is likely, in effect, a much broader license, which would prove extremely difficult to police and contain. Washington's ban on assisting suicide [like Nebraska's ban on partial-birth abortions] prevents such erosion."

Delivery terminates the pregnancy

Now, back to Professor Colb. She is, no doubt, quite aware that the Supreme Court has always defined the abortion liberty as the right of a woman to choose "whether or not to terminate her pregnancy." *Roe.* She also knows that pregnancy cannot be terminated twice. And she concedes, as she must, that partial-birth "abortions" occur after pregnancy has been terminated when she states, "the fetus is literally alive following partial delivery." Because she is unable to overcome the medical fact that the onset of the birth process terminates pregnancy, the professor employs the tactic of equivocation to her purpose in attempting to marginalize the centrality of the fact, saying "[r]hetorically at least, the pregnancy appears to have been terminated without the demise of the fetus." So, the medical fact that fetal demise occurs after pregnancy is terminated in a partial-birth "abortion" is reduced to "rhetoric" and mere "appearance" in the lexicon of Professor Colb.

Because the Court has made it clear that a woman's right to abortion extends only to terminating her pregnancy, the professor attempts to equate the killing of the non-viable infant who is in the process of being born with terminating a pregnancy. This she must do if the procedure is to be brought back under the protective cover of the Court's abortion jurisprudence which has never met an abortion procedure it did not like. Here is the reasoning of our law professor in her own words: "[E]ven with extraordinary medical attention, a 'partially delivered' fetus would live only briefly once removed from the womb, much like a fish removed from water, [therefore] [t]he location of the fetus is effectively inside the womb. And, terminating the pregnancy is synonymous with destroying the fetus." In other words, a non-viable infant in the birth canal is really in the womb, and killing the infant who is in the birth canal is really terminating a pregnancy. Professor Colb fails to explain how, after terminating the pregnancy by pulling the infant into the birth canal, one can terminate the pregnancy again by killing the infant. This is effectively the logic of persecution.

If Professor Colb has her way, we will witness the creation of a new constitutional right even more elastic than the abortion liberty. It will masquerade as abortion, a bad enough thing in itself, but in fact it will be much more because in the world according to Professor Colb, "[v]iability severs [the] conceptual link between terminating a pregnancy and destroying a fetus." According to this logic, the location of the non-viable infant who has been fully delivered is "effectively inside the womb." That is to say, abortionists would be free to "abort" non-viable infants who have been fully delivered because they are, to quote Professor Colb, "effectively inside the womb."

The professor did get one thing right in her article when she said "'partial-birth' abortion cases do not differ in any morally significant way from other legal abortions." The legalized extermination of the most vulnerable and innocent among us, however accomplished, is a tragedy which exceeds the capacity of words to express. But let there be no mistake, the culture of death inaugurated in *Roe* is now in an apoplectic fury as it seeks to extend its grip beyond the womb. There will be a time not too distant when the sick and aged will be considered, as the good professor puts it, "effectively inside the womb."

5

Laws That Prohibit Late-Term Abortion Put Mothers at Risk

Stuart Taylor

Stuart Taylor is a senior writer for the National Journal, *a weekly publication on politics, policy, and government.*

In June 2000, the Supreme Court struck down a Nebraska ban on partial-birth abortions. According to Nebraska's statute, "Partial-birth abortion means an abortion procedure in which the person performing the abortion partially delivers vaginally a living unborn child before killing the unborn child and completing the delivery." Many pro-life advocates argue that partial-birth abortion laws would outlaw a rare and gruesome abortion procedure that takes place after the twenty-fourth week of pregnancy. However, the laws are so vaguely worded that abortions in any stage of pregnancy could be prohibited. Moreover, most partial-birth abortion laws arbitrarily distinguish between whether an aborted fetus is killed in the womb (acceptable) or in the birth canal (criminal). Partial-birth abortion procedures are the safest form of late-term abortion, and restrictions on the procedure endanger the life of the mother.

A ny parent who has rejoiced at seeing a sonogram showing the image of a second-trimester fetus knows how much it looks like a baby. And any parent who has seen a baby blossom into a vibrant teenage girl can imagine the agony of hearing her plead for help in aborting a pregnancy that she had hidden for three months. But any parent who would know with certainty what to say to that teenage girl must be smarter than I am.

Under "partial-birth" abortion laws adopted by many states, twice passed by Congress, and twice vetoed by former president Bill Clinton, one option would apparently be illegal: the most common (by far), and probably the safest, form of second-trimester abortion. That's the basis of three decisions issued on September 24, 1999 by the U.S. Court of Appeals for the 8th Circuit, striking down "partial-birth" abortion laws in Nebraska, Iowa, and Arkansas.

The unanimous 8th Circuit rulings—written by a Carter appointee and joined by two Reagan appointees—are the latest in a line of opinions joined by some 26 judges, including 11 Reagan and Bush appointees, suggesting that "partial-birth" abortion laws are unconstitutional. Four judges thus far have suggested the contrary.

"Partial-birth" abortion laws would ban certain procedures to abort fetuses at any stage of pregnancy.

Right-to-life advocates have sold much of the public, and many legislators, on the myth that "partial-birth" abortion laws would outlaw only an especially grisly (and rare) way of killing third-trimester fetuses on the verge of birth.

False. Some 28 of the 30 state "partial-birth" abortion laws would ban certain procedures to abort fetuses at any stage of pregnancy—including fetuses that are not yet viable, and arguably including some in the first trimester. The laws accept only abortions necessary to protect the life of the woman. And many of them threaten doctors with criminal penalties as harsh as life imprisonment for using abortion procedures that are morally indistinguishable from other procedures that would not be restricted.

Getting the facts

Below I describe two abortion procedures used in the second and third trimesters. Both—indeed, all abortion procedures—are gruesome to contemplate. This may help account for the reluctance of some of us (including me, until now) to ponder in detail whether particular procedures should be banned.

Advocates of "partial-birth" abortion laws claim that they would restrict only an extremely rare procedure called dilation and extraction (D&X). It involves pulling the fetus, feet first, from the uterus, through the cervix, and into the vagina, except for the head; using scissors or another surgical instrument to rupture the skull; and then suctioning out the brain. The more the abortion debate has centered on this image of the dismemberment of nearly born babies—rather than on the plight of women with unwanted pregnancies—the better the right-to-life side has done in the court of public opinion.

Thus was Democratic New York Senator Daniel Patrick Moynihan, for example, persuaded that "partial-birth" abortion is so "close to infanticide" that it should be outlawed. But if Moynihan thought he was voting to restrict only late-term abortions, he was misinformed. As the 8th Circuit held, "partial-birth" abortion has "no fixed legal or medical content." It means whatever a legislature defines it to mean. And under most definitions, these laws are very broad.

The laws in many states, and the measure that passed Congress in 1997, outlaw abortions in which the doctor kills the fetus after pulling any "substantial portion" from the uterus into the vagina.

And that, the 8th Circuit said, is precisely what doctors do, not only in D&X abortions but also in "dilation and evacuation" (D&E) abortions—the most common method in the second trimester. D&E abortions typically involve using forceps to pull an arm or a leg from the uterus into the vagina and then dismembering the fetus.

In striking down the three statutes, the 8th Circuit cited Supreme Court precedents, including the 1992 ruling in *Planned Parenthood vs. Casey* that a state may not place "a substantial obstacle in the path of a woman seeking an abortion" of any fetus that is not yet viable.

In an effort to dodge these precedents, those who defend "partial-birth" abortion laws in court have interpreted them as narrowly as possible, resorting to some bizarre distinctions. Thus, in disputing the view that "partial-birth" abortion laws (or some of them) would restrict D&E abortions, the laws' defenders argue that they would restrict only procedures in which fetuses are intentionally dismembered and killed after being pulled into the vagina (D&X)—and not procedures in which fetuses are dismembered and killed while being pulled into the vagina (D&E).

Think about that distinction

A three-judge panel of the 8th Circuit showed that the Nebraska, Iowa, and Arkansas statutes in fact make no such distinction. Written by Judge Richard S. Arnold—a Carter appointee (and Little Rock friend of former president Clinton's)—the three 8th Circuit opinions were joined by Chief Judge Roger L. Wollman of the 8th Circuit and Chief Judge Paul A. Magnuson of the U.S. District Court in Minnesota. Both are Reagan appointees.

The 8th Circuit left it to others to ponder why, as a matter of morality or common sense, the legality of an abortion should turn on where in the birth canal various parts of the fetus are located when it is killed.

Chief Judge Richard A. Posner of the U.S. Court of Appeals for the 7th Circuit tackled that question in November 1998 in a decision that preliminarily enjoined Wisconsin's "partial-birth" abortion statute.

"The constitutional right to an abortion carries with it the right to perform medical procedures that many people find distasteful or worse," wrote Posner, a Reagan appointee. "The singling out of the D&X procedure for anathematization seems arbitrary to the point of irrationality. Annexing the penalty of life imprisonment to a medical procedure that may be the safest alternative for women who have chosen abortion because of the risk that childbirth would pose to their health adds a note of the macabre to the Wisconsin statute."

Senseless distinctions

I'm with Posner. I can well understand why some critics of *Roe* want to outlaw any procedure that destroys a fetus, especially in the later stages of pregnancy. I can't understand why the legality of an abortion should not turn on the safety of the procedure, or the health of the woman, or the stage of fetal development—but rather on exactly how far into the birth canal the fetus is pulled before being destroyed.

"No argument is made," as Posner wrote, "that if a fetus feels pain, the pain feels worse when the fetus is killed in the birth canal than when death occurs a moment earlier in the womb."

Posner also punctured the implausible claims that "partial-birth" abortion laws don't burden women seeking abortions, because an equally safe, legal alternative procedure is always available. If this were so, Posner wrote, the statute "cannot discourage abortions—cannot save any fetuses—but can merely shift their locus from the birth canal to the uterus."

Conversely, such a law "can save fetuses only by endangering pregnant women, since the only time a woman denied a "partial birth" abortion will decide to carry the fetus to term is when the alternative methods of abortion would pose a greater risk to her."

And if (as some evidence suggests) "partial-birth" abortion laws, in fact, would block some women from access to the safest abortion procedure, the laws also conflict with *Roe*'s holding that even post-viability abortions may not be restricted in ways that would endanger the woman's life or health (including emotional health).

None of this is in the Constitution, of course. That's why *Roe* is so hard to defend as an exercise in constitutional interpretation. But even if the Supreme Court was wrong to constitutionalize abortion in 1973, the question on the table is whether "partial-birth" abortion laws make any sense now.

To return to where I started: If I had a daughter who (after due consideration of all options) wanted a second-trimester abortion, I'd probably swallow my misgivings and help her get one. If the safest abortion procedure were illegal where we lived, I'd take her to another state, or another country. If the fetus were viable, I might feel differently. But even then, my main concern would be my daughter's health, including her mental health.

That's why I would not support a "partial-birth" abortion law, even if it was limited to viable fetuses—and why I see no sense in these laws as written, most of which would deny the safest abortion procedure to women at earlier stages of pregnancy.

6

Roe v. Wade Must Be Overturned

Peter Kreeft

Peter Kreeft is a professor of philosophy at Boston College. He has written several books, including Three Approaches to Abortion *and* The Unaborted Socrates.

The 1973 Supreme Court decision that legalized abortion, *Roe v. Wade*, must be overturned. Socratic logic suggests that if people know what an apple is, then they know what human beings are. If people know what human beings are, then they know that all human beings are entitled to human rights, simply because they are human. By this logic, abortion is wrong because pre-born humans are entitled to the same human rights that already-born humans enjoy. This conclusion is based upon the assumptions that life begins at conception, that all humans have a right to life, and that the law must protect human rights. Pro-choice advocates who disagree with this conclusion must be scientifically, morally, or legally ignorant.

I doubt there are many readers of *Crisis* who are pro-choice. Why, then, do I write an argument against abortion for its readers? Why preach to the choir?

Preaching to the choir is a legitimate enterprise. Scripture calls it "edification," or "building up." It is what priests, ministers, rabbis, and mullahs try to do once every week. We all need to clean and improve our apologetic weapons periodically; and this argument is the most effective one I know for actual use in dialogue with intelligent pro-choicers.

I will be as upfront as possible. I will try to prove the simple, common-sensical reasonableness of the pro-life case by a sort of Socratic logic. My conclusion is that *Roe v. Wade* must be overturned, and my fundamental reason for this is not only because of what abortion is but because *we all know* what abortion is.

This is obviously a controversial conclusion, and initially unacceptable to all pro-choicers. So, my starting point must be noncontroversial.

It is this: We know what an apple is. I will try to persuade you that if we know what an apple is, *Roe v. Wade* must be overthrown, and that if you want to defend *Roe*, you will probably want to deny that we know what an apple is.

We know what an apple is

Our first principle should be as undeniable as possible, for arguments usually go back to their first principles. If we find our first premise to be a stone wall that cannot be knocked down when we back up against it, our argument will be strong. Tradition states and common sense dictates our premise that we know what an apple is. Almost no one doubted this, until quite recently. Even now, only philosophers, scholars, "experts," media mavens, professors, journalists, and mind-molders dare to claim that we do not know what an apple is.

We really know what an apple really is

From the premise that "we know what an apple is," I move to a second principle that is only an explication of the meaning of the first: that we *really* know what an apple *really* is. If this is denied, our first principle is refuted. It becomes, "We know, but not really, what an apple is, but not really." Step 2 says only, "Let us not 'nuance' Step 1 out of existence!"

We really know what some things really are

From Step 2, I deduce the third principle, also as an immediate logical corollary, that we really know what some things (other things than apples) really are. This follows if we only add the minor premise that an apple is another thing.

This third principle, of course, is the repudiation of skepticism. The secret has been out since Socrates that skepticism is logically self-contradictory. To say "I do not know" is to say "I know I do not know." Socrates's wisdom was not skepticism. He was not the only man in the world who knew that he did not know. He had knowledge; he did not claim to have wisdom. He knew he *was* not wise. That is a wholly different affair and is not self-contradictory. All forms of skepticism are logically self-contradictory, nuance as we will.

If we know what an apple is, Roe v. Wade *must be overthrown.*

All talk about rights, about right and wrong, about justice, presupposes this principle that we really know what some things really are. We cannot argue about anything at all—anything real, as distinct from arguing about arguing, and about words, and attitudes—unless we accept this principle. We can talk about feelings without it, but we cannot talk about justice. We can have a reign of feelings—or a reign of terror—without it, but we cannot have a reign of law.

We know what human beings are

Our fourth principle is that we know what we are, if we know what an apple is, surely we know what a human being is. For we aren't apples; we don't live as apples, we don't feel what apples feel (if anything). We don't experience the existence or growth or life of apples, yet we know what apples are. A *fortiori*, we know what we are, for we have "inside information," privileged information, more and better information.

We have human rights because we are human beings.

We obviously do not have total, or even adequate, knowledge of ourselves, or of apples, or (if we listen to Thomas Aquinas) of even a flea. There is obviously more mystery in a human than in an apple, but there is also more knowledge. I repeat this point because I know it is often not understood: To claim that "we know what we are" is not to claim that we know all that we are, or even that we know *adequately* or *completely* or *with full understanding anything at all* of what we are. We are a living mystery, but we also *know* much of this mystery. Knowledge and mystery are no more incompatible than eating and hungering for more.

We have human rights because we are human

The fifth principle is the indispensable, common-sensical basis for human rights: We have human rights because we are human beings.

We have not yet said *what* human beings are (e.g., do we have souls?), or *what* human rights are (e.g., do we have the right to "life, liberty, and the pursuit of happiness?"), only the simple point that we have *whatever* human rights we have because we are *whatever* it is that makes us human.

This certainly sounds innocent enough, but it implies a general principle. Let's call that our sixth principle.

Morality is based on metaphysics

Metaphysics means simply philosophizing about reality. The sixth principle means that rights depend on reality, and our knowledge of rights depends on our knowledge of reality.

By this point in our argument, some are probably feeling impatient. These impatient ones are common-sensical people, uncorrupted by the chattering classes. They will say, "Of course. We know all this. Get on with it. Get to the controversial stuff." Ah, but I suspect we began with the controversial stuff. For not all are impatient; others are uneasy. "Too simplistic," "not nuanced," "a complex issue"—do these phrases leap to mind as shields to protect you from the spear that you know is coming at the end of the argument?

The principle that morality depends on metaphysics means that rights depend on reality, or what is *right* depends on what *is*. Even if you say you are skeptical of metaphysics, we all do use the principle in moral or legal arguments. For instance, in the current debate about "animal rights," some of us think that animals do have rights and some of us think they don't, but we all agree that if they do have rights, they have animal rights, not human rights or plant rights, because they are animals, not humans or plants. For instance, a dog doesn't have the right to vote, as humans do, because dogs are not rational, as humans are. But a dog probably does have a right not to be tortured. Why? Because of what a dog is, and because we really know a little bit about what a dog really is: We really know that a dog feels pain and a tree doesn't. Dogs have feelings, unlike trees, and dogs don't have reason, like humans; that's why it's wrong to break a limb off a dog but it's not wrong to break a limb off a tree, and that's also why dogs don't have the right to vote but humans do.

Moral arguments presuppose metaphysical principles

The main reason people deny that morality must (or even can) be based on metaphysics is that they say we don't really know what reality is, we only have opinions. They point out, correctly, that we are less agreed about morality than science or everyday practical facts. We don't differ about whether the sun is a planet or whether we need to eat to live, but we do differ about things like abortion, capital punishment, and animal rights.

But the very fact that we argue about it—a fact the skeptic points to as a reason for skepticism—is a refutation of skepticism. We don't argue about how we feel, about subjective things. You never hear an argument like this: "I feel great." "No, I feel terrible."

Harming or killing another against his will . . . is clearly wrong.

For instance, both pro-lifers and pro-choicers usually agree that it's wrong to kill innocent persons against their will and it's not wrong to kill parts of persons, like cancer cells. And both the proponents and opponents of capital punishment usually agree that human life is of great value; that's why the proponent wants to protect the life of the innocent by executing murderers and why the opponent wants to protect the life even of the murderer. They radically disagree about how to apply the principle that human life is valuable, but they both assume and appeal to that same principle.

Might making right

All these examples so far are controversial. How to *apply* moral principles to these issues is controversial. What is not controversial, I hope, is the principle itself that human rights are possessed by human beings because of what they are, because of their being—and not because some other human beings have the power to enforce their will. That would be, literally, "might makes right." Instead of putting might into the hands of right, that would be pinning the label of "right" on the face of might: justifying force instead of fortifying justice. But that is the only alternative, no matter what the political power structure, no matter who or how many hold the power, whether a single tyrant, or an aristocracy, or a majority of the freely voting public, or the vague sentiment of what Jean-Jacques Rousseau called "the general will." The political form does not change the principle. A constitutional monarchy, in which the king and the people are subject to the same law, is a rule of law, not of power; a lawless democracy, in which the will of the majority is unchecked, is a rule of power, not of law.

Either all have rights or only some have rights

The reason all human beings have human rights is that all human beings are human. Only two philosophies of human rights are logically possible. Either all human beings have rights, or only some human beings have rights. There is no third possibility. But the *reason* for believing either one of these two possibilities is even more important than which one you believe.

Suppose you believe that all human beings have rights. Do you believe that all human beings have rights *because they are human beings*? Do you dare to do metaphysics? Are human rights "inalienable" because they are inherent in human nature, in the human essence, in the human being, in what humans, in fact, are? Or do you believe that all human beings have rights *because some human beings say so*—because some human wills have declared that all human beings have rights? If it's the first reason, you are secure against tyranny and usurpation of rights. If it's the second reason, you are not. For human nature doesn't change, but human wills do. The same human wills that say today that all humans have rights may well say tomorrow that only some have rights.

Why abortion is wrong

Some people want to be killed. I won't address the morality of voluntary euthanasia here. But clearly, *involuntary* euthanasia is wrong; clearly, there is a difference between imposing power on another and freely making a contract with another. The contract may still be a bad one, a contract to do a wrong thing, and the mere fact that the parties to the contract entered it freely does not automatically justify doing the thing they contract to do. But harming or killing another against his will, not by free contract, is clearly wrong; if that isn't wrong, what is?

But that's what abortion is. Mother Teresa argued, simply, "If abortion is not wrong, nothing is wrong." The fetus doesn't want to be killed; it seeks to escape. Did you dare to watch *The Silent Scream*? Did the media dare to allow it to be shown? No, they will censor nothing except the most common operation in America.

The argument from the nonexistence of nonpersons

Are persons a subclass of humans, or are humans a subclass of persons? The issue of distinguishing humans and persons comes up only for two reasons: the possibility that there are nonhuman persons, like extraterrestrials, elves, angels, gods, God, or the Persons of the Trinity, or the possibility that there are some nonpersonal humans, unpersons, humans without rights.

Traditional common sense and morality say all humans are persons and have rights. Modern moral relativism says that only some humans are persons, for only those who are given rights by others (i.e., those in power) have rights. Thus, if we have power, we can "depersonalize" any group we want: blacks, slaves, Jews, political enemies, liberals, fundamentalists—or unborn babies.

A common way to state this philosophy is the claim that membership in a biological species confers no rights. I have heard it argued that we do not treat any other species in the traditional way—that is, we do not assign equal rights to all mice. Some we kill (those that get into our houses and prove to be pests); others we take good care of and preserve (those that we find useful in laboratory experiments or those we adopt as pets); still others we simply ignore (mice in the wild). The argument concludes that therefore, it is only sentiment or tradition (the two are often confused, as if nothing rational could be passed down by tradition) that assigns rights to all members of our own species.

Three pro-life premises and three pro-choice alternatives

We have been assuming three premises, and they are the three fundamental assumptions of the pro-life argument. Any one of them can be denied. To be pro-choice, you *must* deny at least one of them, because taken together they logically entail the pro-life conclusion. But there are three different kinds of pro-choice positions, depending on which of the three pro-life premises is denied.

The first premise is scientific, the second is moral, and the third is legal. The scientific premise is that the life of the individual member of every animal species begins at conception. (This truism was taught by all biology textbooks before *Roe* and by none after *Roe*; yet *Roe* did not discover or appeal to any new scientific discoveries.) In other words, all humans are human, whether embryonic, fetal, infantile, young, mature, old, or dying.

> *The law must protect the right to life of all humans.*

The moral premise is that all humans have the right to life because all humans are human. It is a deduction from the most obvious of all moral rules, the Golden Rule, or justice, or equality. If you would not be killed, do not kill. It's just not just, not fair. All humans have the human essence and, therefore, are essentially equal.

The legal premise is that the law must protect the most basic human rights. If all humans are human, and if all humans have a right to life, and if the law must protect human rights, then the law must protect the right to life of all humans.

If all three premises are true, the pro-life conclusion follows. From the pro-life point of view, there are only three reasons for being pro-choice: scientific ignorance—appalling ignorance of a scientific fact so basic that nearly everyone in the world knows it; moral ignorance—appalling ignorance of the most basic of all moral rules; or legal ignorance—appalling ignorance of one of the most basic of all the functions of law. But there are significant differences among these different kinds of ignorance.

Roe *used such skepticism to justify a pro-choice position.*

Scientific ignorance, if it is not *ignoring*, or deliberate denial or dishonesty, is perhaps pitiable but not morally blame-worthy. You don't have to be wicked to be stupid. If you believe an unborn baby is only "potential life" or a "group of cells," then you do not believe you are killing a human being when you abort and might have no qualms of conscience about it. (But why, then, do most mothers who abort feel such terrible pangs of conscience, often for a lifetime?)

Most pro-choice arguments, during the first two decades after *Roe*, disputed the *scientific* premise of the pro-life argument. It might be that this was almost always dishonest rather than honest ignorance, but perhaps not, and at least it didn't directly deny the essential second premise, the *moral* principle. But pro-choice arguments today increasingly do.

Perhaps pro-choicers perceive that they have no choice but to do this, for they have no other recourse if they are to argue at all. Scientific facts are just too clear to deny, and it makes no legal sense to deny the legal principle, for if the law is not supposed to defend the right to life, what is it supposed to do? So they have to deny the moral principle that leads to the pro-life conclusion. This, I suspect, is a vast and major sea change. The camel has gotten not just his nose, but his torso under the tent. I think most people refuse to think or argue about abortion because they see that the only way to remain pro-choice is to abort their reason first. Or, since many pro-choicers insist that abortion is about sex, not about babies, the only way to justify their scorn of virginity is a scorn of intellectual virginity. The only way to justify their loss of moral innocence is to lose their intellectual innocence.

If the above paragraph offends you, I challenge you to calmly and honestly ask your own conscience and reason whether, where, and why it is false.

The argument from skepticism

The most likely response to this will be the charge of dogmatism. How dare I pontificate with infallible certainty, and call all who disagree either mentally or morally challenged! All right, here is an argument even for the metaphysical skeptic, who would not even agree with my very first and simplest premise, that we really do know what some things really are, such as what an apple is. (It's only after you are pinned against the wall and have to justify something like abortion that you become a skeptic and deny such a self-evident principle.)

Roe used such skepticism to justify a pro-choice position. Since we don't know when human life begins, the argument went, we cannot impose restrictions. (Why it is more restrictive to give life than to take it, I cannot figure out.) So here is my refutation of *Roe* on its own premises, its skeptical premises: Suppose that not a single principle of this essay is true, beginning with the first one. Suppose that we do not even know what an apple is. Even then abortion is unjustifiable.

I honestly wish a pro-choicer would someday show me one argument that proved that fetuses are not persons.

Let's assume not a dogmatic skepticism (which is self-contradictory) but a skeptical skepticism. Let us also assume that we do not know whether a fetus is a person or not. In objective fact, of course, either it is or it isn't (unless the Court has revoked the Law of Noncontradiction while we were on vacation), but in our subjective minds, we may not know what the fetus is in objective fact. We do know, however, that either it is or isn't by formal logic alone.

A second thing we know by formal logic alone is that either we do or do not know what a fetus is. Either there is "out there," in objective fact, independent of our minds, a human life, or there is not; and either there is knowledge in our minds of this objective fact, or there is not.

So, there are four possibilities:
1. The fetus is a person, and we know that;
2. The fetus is a person, but we don't know that;
3. The fetus isn't a person, but we don't know that;
4. The fetus isn't a person, and we know that. What is abortion in each of these four cases?

In Case 1, where the fetus is a person *and you know that*, abortion is murder. First-degree murder, in fact. You deliberately kill an innocent human being.

In Case 2, where the fetus is a person and you *don't* know that, abortion is manslaughter. It's like driving over a man-shaped overcoat in the street at night or shooting toxic chemicals into a building that you're not sure is fully evacuated. You're not sure there is a person there, but you're not sure there isn't either, and it just so happens that there is a person there, and you kill him. You cannot plead ignorance. True, you didn't know there was a person there, but you didn't know there *wasn't* either, so your act was literally the height of irresponsibility. This is the act *Roe* allowed.

In Case 3, the fetus isn't a person, *but you don't know that*. So abortion is just as irresponsible as it is in the previous case. You ran over the overcoat or fumigated the building without knowing that there were no persons there. You were lucky; there weren't. But you didn't care; you didn't take care; you were just as irresponsible. You cannot legally be charged with manslaughter, since no man was slaughtered, but you can and should be charged with criminal negligence.

Only in Case 4 is abortion a reasonable, permissible, and responsible choice. But note: What makes Case 4 permissible is not merely the fact that the fetus is not a person but also your knowledge that it is not, your overcoming of skepticism. So skepticism counts not for abortion but against it. Only if you are not a skeptic, only if you are a dogmatist, only if you are certain that there is no person in the fetus, no man in the coat, or no person in the building, may you abort, drive, or fumigate.

This undercuts even our weakest, least honest escape: to pretend that we don't even know what an apple is, just so we have an excuse for pleading that we don't know what an abortion is.

One last plea

I hope a reader can show me where I've gone astray in the sequence of 13 steps that constitute this argument. I honestly wish a pro-choicer would someday show me one argument that proved that fetuses are not persons. It would save me and other pro-lifers enormous grief, time, effort, worry, prayers, and money. But until that time, I will keep arguing, because it's what I do as a philosopher. It is my weak and wimpy version of a mother's shouting that something terrible is happening: Babies are being slaughtered. I will do this because, as Edmund Burke declared, "The only thing necessary for the triumph of evil is that good men do nothing."

7

Roe v. Wade Must Be Upheld

National Abortion Rights Action League

The National Abortion Rights Action League is a nonprofit organization that works toward establishing more effective contraceptive options, better access to other kinds of reproductive health care and information, and reducing the need for abortions while maintaining a woman's right to choose.

The Supreme Court's 1973 decision to legalize abortion, *Roe v. Wade*, established that a woman's right to choose abortion fell under the constitutionally protected right to privacy. While recognizing a woman's right to privacy, *Roe* also protected the rights of the fetus by banning elective abortion after viability. *Roe* has protected the lives of thousands of women who may otherwise have risked their lives by obtaining medically-unsafe back-alley abortions. Despite the constitutionality of the *Roe* decision, since 1992, the Supreme Court has enacted several restrictions on abortion rights that were previously considered violations of the right to privacy. *Roe v. Wade* must be upheld to ensure a woman's right to choose.

> "At the heart of liberty is the right to define one's own concept of existence, of meaning, of the universe, and of the mystery of human life. Beliefs about these matters could not define the attributes of personhood were they formed under compulsion of the State."
>
> —U.S. Supreme Court Justices O'Connor, Kennedy and Souter, *Planned Parenthood of Southeastern Pennsylvania v. Casey*

Abortion in the United States before *Roe*

When *Roe v. Wade* was decided in January 1973, abortion except to save a woman's life was banned in nearly two-thirds of the states. Laws in most of the remaining states contained only a few additional exceptions. An estimated 1.2 million women each year resorted to illegal

44

abortion, despite the known hazards "of frightening trips to dangerous lo-
cations in strange parts of town; of whiskey as an anesthetic; of 'doctors'
who were often marginal or unlicensed practitioners, sometimes alco-
holic, sometimes sexually abusive; unsanitary conditions; incompetent
treatment; infection; hemorrhage; disfiguration; and death" according to
Walter Dellinger and Gene B. Sperling in their article "Abortion and the
Supreme Court: The Retreat from *Roe* v. *Wade*."

The constitutional development of the right to privacy

During the half century leading up to *Roe*, the Supreme Court decided a
series of significant cases in which it recognized the existence of a constitutionally protected right to privacy that keeps fundamentally important
and deeply personal decisions concerning "bodily integrity, identity and
destiny" largely beyond the reach of government interference as stated in
Planned Parenthood v. Casey. Citing this concern for autonomy and privacy, the Court struck down laws severely curtailing the role of parents in
education, mandating sterilization, and prohibiting marriages between
individuals of different races.

---

*By invalidating laws that forced women to resort to
back-alley abortion,* Roe *was directly responsible for
saving women's lives.*

Important aspects of the right to privacy were established in *Griswold
v. Connecticut*, decided in 1965, and in *Eisenstadt v. Baird*, decided in 1972.
In these cases, the Supreme Court held that state laws that criminalized
or hindered the use of contraception violated the right to privacy. Having recognized in these cases "the right of the individual to be free from
unwarranted governmental intrusion into matters so fundamentally affecting a person as the decision whether to bear or beget a child," according to *Eisenstadt v. Baird*, the Court held in *Roe* that the right to privacy encompasses the right to choose whether to end a pregnancy.

The Court has reaffirmed this holding on multiple occasions throughout the past 27 years, noting in *Casey* 1992 that "[t]he soundness of this
. . . analysis is apparent from a consideration of the alternative." Without
a privacy right that encompasses the right to choose, the Constitution
would permit the state to override not only a woman's decision to terminate her pregnancy, but also her choice to carry the pregnancy to term.

Although *Roe* invalidated restrictive abortion laws that disregarded
women's right to privacy, the Court recognized a state's valid interest in
potential life. That is, the Court rejected arguments that the right to
choose is absolute and always outweighs the state's interest in imposing
limitations. Instead, the Court issued a carefully crafted decision that
brought the state's interest and the woman's right to choose into balance.

The Court held that a woman has the right to choose abortion until
fetal viability, but that the state's interest generally outweighs the woman's right after that point. Accordingly, after viability—the time at which
it first becomes realistically possible for fetal life to be maintained outside

the woman's body—the state may ban any abortion not necessary to preserve a woman's life or health.

A better life for women

By invalidating laws that forced women to resort to back-alley abortion, *Roe* was directly responsible for saving women's lives. As many as 5000 women died yearly from illegal abortion before *Roe*. Since the legalization of abortion in 1973, the safety of abortion has increased dramatically. The number of deaths per 100,000 legal abortion procedures declined more than five-fold between 1973 and 1991. In addition, *Roe* has had a positive impact on the quality of many women's lives. Although most women welcome pregnancy, childbirth and the responsibilities of raising a child at some period in their lives, few events can more dramatically constrain a woman's opportunities than an unplanned child. Because childbirth and pregnancy substantially affect a woman's "educational prospects, employment opportunities, and self-determination," as stated in *Casey*, restrictive abortion laws narrowly circumscribed women's role in society and hindered women from defining their paths through life in the most basic of ways. In the years since *Roe*, the variety and level of women's achievements have reached unprecedented levels. The Supreme Court recently observed in *Casey* that "[t]he ability of women to participate equally in the economic and social life of the Nation has been facilitated by their ability to control their reproductive lives."

Into the new millennium

In 1992, the Court rendered its most important decision in the abortion area since *Roe*. In *Planned Parenthood of Southeastern Pennsylvania v. Casey*, the Court reaffirmed *Roe*, while at the same time sharply restricting its protections. The *Casey* Court abandoned the strict scrutiny standard of review and adopted a less protective standard that allows states to impose restrictions as long as they do not "unduly burden" a woman's right to choose. Under this new standard, the Court approved state obstacles that it had previously found to violate the right to privacy and effectively invited states to impose barriers on women's access to abortion. Indeed, under *Casey's* looser standard, the Court has allowed a multitude of state restrictions to be imposed upon reproductive freedom and choice.

It seems inevitable that great strides will be made in this millennium in science, technology, athletics, communication, and in numerous other fields of human endeavor. What is less clear is whether proponents of women's reproductive health and freedom will be able to move forward in the 21st century—to secure better access to effective methods of contraception, comprehensive sexuality education, and quality health and child care—or will remain locked in a struggle against further deterioration of the right to choose ostensibly secured by *Roe* more than a quarter century ago.

In June, 2000, the Supreme Court issued its most significant ruling on abortion rights since *Casey*. While emphatically maintaining the centrality of women's health and striking down Nebraska's ban on safe, common abortion procedures, the Court's ruling in *Stenberg v. Carhart* was won by the slimmest of margins. If even one more pro-choice voice is lost on the Court, states will be free to enact sweeping abortion bans that fail to protect women's health.

It is past time for the nation to develop policies that secure access to abortion, make abortion less necessary, and improve reproductive health. Our nation must commit resources to prevent unintended pregnancy by promoting sexuality education, family planning and healthy childbearing. Only then will the promise of *Roe* be fulfilled.

8

Parental-Involvement Laws Protect Teens

Spencer Abraham and Ileana Ros-Lehtinen

Spencer Abraham, who served as senator from Michigan from 1995 to 2001, is the Secretary of Energy. Ileana Ros-Lehtinen, the first Hispanic woman elected to Congress, is a former senator and a Republican representative from Miami.

In 1996, a thirteen-year-old girl was impregnated by an eighteen-year-old man in a small town in Pennsylvania. Since Pennsylvania requires minors to get the consent of at least one parent before undergoing an abortion, the young man's mother drove the girl to New York for an abortion without the girl's mother's knowledge. The young man's mother was charged and convicted of interference with the custody of a minor, and the young man was convicted of statutory rape. This case inspired the House of Representatives to pass the Child Custody Protection Act in 1998, which would enforce parental-involvement laws and stiffen penalties against anyone who transports a minor across state lines to avoid such laws. Parental-involvement laws protect parents' rights to know about the important decisions that their children face. The act is being reviewed by the Senate.

Rosa Marie Hartford had a problem. Her 18-year-old son had had sex with a local 13-year-old, and the girl had gotten pregnant. This was serious business, especially in the small town of Shunk, Pennsylvania, where she lived.

Hartford's son, Michael Kilmer, could be charged with rape, statutory rape and corruption of a minor. Her family's reputation could be ruined (not to mention the damage to the young neighbor girl's reputation and her relationship with her family). If the girl chose to have the baby, everyone would know she had gotten pregnant (including the authorities), and Hartford's son would be in deep trouble.

And, even if the girl chose to have an abortion, the cat would be out of the bag because Pennsylvania requires minors to get the consent of at least one parent (or a judge) before undergoing an abortion. What was a mother to do?

Hartford was not out of options. She did not have to bring the girl's parents in on the situation. Instead, she put the girl into her own daughter's car, and had a friend (an adult male) drive her and the girl to an abortion clinic 60 miles away, across the state line in Binghampton, New York, a state without any parental-involvement requirement.

Unfortunately for Hartford and her son, the secret abortion did not remain secret. The girl's mother became concerned on seeing a note on her daughter's bed. She contacted her daughter's school and found out that she was not in class. The mother heard several rumors as to her daughter's whereabouts.

Before she knew it, Hartford was being charged with interfering with the custody of a child. Her son pled guilty to statutory rape.

Thousands of pregnant girls are taken across state lines by adults to obtain secret abortions.

The most shocking thing about this story is just how common it is. At least 22 states have parental-involvement laws in effect. Yet, according to the pro-abortion Center for Reproductive Law & Policy (CRLP), thousands of pregnant girls are taken across state lines by adults to obtain secret abortions, thereby circumventing these laws.

A veritable secret abortion industry has grown up to take care of the demand. Abortion clinics in states without parental-involvement laws (such as New York and New Jersey) now take out large advertisements in the Yellow Pages of cities like Harrisburg, Pennsylvania, proudly proclaiming "no parental consent." And now certain pro-abortion groups are claiming a constitutional right to procure secret abortions for minors.

Hartford told the *Wilkes-Barre Times Leader*, "I don't feel guilty of anything. I'm not a criminal. I was helping out." The CRLP agrees. That organization defended Hartford on the grounds that she merely "assisted a woman to exercise her constitutional rights" and so was protected from prosecution by the Supreme Court's decision in *Roe v. Wade*.

In essence, the CRLP is claiming that, because *Roe v. Wade* made most abortions legal during the first trimester, minors must have an unfettered right to abortion on demand, and anyone who wishes may help children obtain secret abortions at any time without fear of prosecution. After all, said the CRLP's Kathryn Kolbert, "How does a 14-year-old get to New Hampshire [where there is no parental-involvement requirement] from Boston [where such a requirement exists] without getting a ride?"

How? She talks to her parents.

The integrity of the family

Whatever one's position on abortion, every American should recognize the crucial role of parents in their minor child's decision whether or not to undergo an abortion. In fact, 74% of Americans in a 1996 Gallup poll favored requiring women under 18 to get parental consent for an abortion. The American people quite reasonably believe that the decision of whether to abort a child is so serious and life changing that no child should have to make it alone. As the Supreme Court noted in *H.L. v. Matheson,* "The medical, emotional, and psychological consequences of an abortion are serious and can be lasting; this is particularly so when the patient is immature."

We must protect family from purveyors of secret abortions.

Let us consider the situation in which the 13-year-old girl in Pennsylvania found herself. An 18-year-old man had gotten her pregnant. He was understandably frightened of legal sanctions. She was facing public embarrassment and stigma. She also was understandably reluctant to inform her mother that she had become sexually active at such a young age, and with an adult. No matter how good her relations with her mother (and they might not be that good), she might at least be tempted to simply put the embarrassing pregnancy to an end.

Under these conditions, a neighbor woman, even the mother of the man responsible for getting her pregnant, may look as if she is just "helping out" by helping to take her to another state for a secret abortion.

But, as most Americans realize, this is no solution. The pain and mental anguish of the child will be no less because she did not share it with her parents. There will always be the knowledge that, had she consulted her parents, she might have brought her baby to term, either to be put up for adoption by a loving family or to be brought up as part of the family to which she already belonged. And the trust between parents and child so crucial to any proper upbringing will be broken, perhaps beyond repair.

By allowing this to happen, we have not "freed" a child from onerous constraints. We have stripped from her the natural protection of her parents.

Parental-notification and consent laws exist for a reason. While most such laws provide for a possible judicial bypass, they by nature intend to protect the rights and integrity of the family. Without a good upbringing, any child will be at significantly increased risk of drug abuse, crime, poverty and even suicide. That is why it is crucial that we protect, as much as we possibly can, the rights of American parents to be involved in all important decisions affecting their children. Only by being a part of their lives can parents provide their children with the guidance they need and maintain the mutual trust necessary to teach them how to lead good, productive lives.

That is why we must protect families from purveyors of secret abortions, whatever their motives. Children must receive parental consent for even minor surgical procedures. The profound, lasting physical and psychological effects of abortion demand that we help states guarantee parental involvement in the abortion decision.

That means, at a minimum, seeing to it that outside parties cannot circumvent state parental notification and consent laws with impunity. Congress is considering our legislation, the "Child Custody Protection Act," aimed at enforcing state parental notification laws. It would make anyone who transports a minor across state lines to circumvent such a law guilty of a misdemeanor and liable to be fined and/or jailed for up to one year. We believe children and their families—as well as our society as a whole—need and deserve this protection.

We must protect the rule of law against those who would undermine it in the name of unfettered abortion rights. We must protect our constitutional order against those who would stretch rights so far beyond their rational bounds as to call all of them into question. We must protect children against people who, for whatever reason, seek to tear them away from their parents as they make a life-changing decision. And we must protect our families from anyone who would interfere with their fundamental role in shaping good character and providing a sound basis for our lives, as individuals and as a community.

9

Parental-Involvement Laws Violate Women's Rights

Amy Bach

Amy Bach is a clerk for the U.S. Court of Appeals for the Eleventh Circuit in Miami, Florida.

A 1992 Supreme Court decision mandated that a state may require a young woman under the age of eighteen to either obtain her parents' consent to have an abortion or the consent of a judge. Most states have since enacted a parental-involvement law, and these laws have made it extremely difficult for a young woman to exercise her right to choose an abortion. In many cases, young women face staunchly pro-life judges, some of whom appoint an attorney to represent the fetus. Parental-involvement laws are wrong because they support the rights of the unborn over the rights of the mother.

In 1992, in *Planned Parenthood v. Casey*, the Supreme Court ruled that a state may require a young woman who wants an abortion to obtain her parents' consent—as long as there is a "bypass procedure" that allows her to apply for consent from a judge instead. At the time, abortion rights advocates bemoaned the *Casey* decision for severely narrowing the scope of *Roe v. Wade*, but few could have imagined just how paper-thin young women's right to choose might soon become.

In many of the forty-two states that now have parental notification laws (including New Jersey, signed into law by "pro-choice" Governor Christine Todd Whitman), antiabortion judges have been highly creative when faced with pregnant minors who want their consent for abortions: using harassing interrogation tactics, appointing antichoice attorneys to represent the young women, and even—in a few cases whose implications are still unfolding—assigning lawyers to represent the interests of fetuses.

Juvenile Judge Mark Anderson in Montgomery, Alabama, has made no secret of his antiabortion proclivities, explaining in written decisions his "fixed opinion that abortion is wrong" and routinely denying parental consent waivers because the young women hadn't proved their

Parental-Involvement Laws Violate Women's Rights

"maturity" (the standard mandated by *Casey*). He is quite clear that demonstrating maturity in his courtroom means accepting his view of abortion. In denying consent to a 16-year-old, he wrote, "She goes to church but she testified that she had not considered the spiritual aspects of her decision." Judge Anderson also found that although she did receive counseling from a reproductive health clinic on the medical risks of abortion and assistance available to unwed mothers, she had not "sought counseling from a group or facility which opposes abortion. . . . would it not be more convincing evidence of her maturity if she had . . . on her own . . . gone to hear the other side?"

Pro-choice advocates across the country can rattle off the names of juvenile judges they advise girls to avoid.

It was in another case, involving a 17-year-old, that Judge Anderson decided to appoint a lawyer to represent the fetus. The judge explained that he wanted to give the "unborn child" a "guardian ad litem" (an agent of the court usually appointed to represent children's interests) to assure that the fetus had "an opportunity to have a voice, even a vicarious one, in the decision making."

The young woman's own court-appointed lawyer had carefully prepped her client, a high school honors student who had a scholarship for college. She told the court that she believed abortion was a sin, that if any complications arose she realized that it would be God's punishment and that she had sought counseling with a group called Sav-A-Life, where she had cradled a rubber fetus doll in her hands. She explained that she could not ask her mother for consent because her mother had told her that if she ever got pregnant she could not live at home and would receive no help. She also feared violence from her father, who had been known to point a gun at boys who looked at her provocatively.

Enter the fetus's guardian, Montgomery attorney Julian McPhillips, who had given his "client" a name, "Baby Ashley." Over numerous constitutional objections by the young woman's counsel, according to transcripts of the closed hearing, McPhillips proceeded methodically. "You say that you are aware that God instructed you not to kill your own baby, but you want to do it anyway? And are you saying here today that notwithstanding everything that you want to interfere with God's plan for your baby?"

"I think that is between me and God," she said.

McPhillips continued. "And you are not concerned after you have had the abortion that some day you may wake up and say my gosh, what have I done to my own baby?"

"It may happen," she said.

"You are not worried about being haunted by this? Here you have the chance to save the life of your own baby. . . . And still you want to go ahead and snuff out the life of your own baby?"

"Yes."

After four hours of what Judge Anderson called "argument of the most acrimonious nature," he made the "regretful" finding that the girl was indeed well informed. The Alabama Court of Appeals denied an appeal from McPhillips on Baby Ashley's behalf, on the basis that only the young woman could appeal. The girl obtained the abortion, but she still regards her experience with Judge Anderson as a horrible ordeal. "He's a son of a bitch," she told her lawyer.

When the local press heard about Judge Anderson's new guardian-ad-litem policy, it ran news stories and uncomplimentary editorials, and judicial higher-ups stopped assigning parental consent cases to him. But his tactics won him a following among antiabortion activists, and Alabama legislators soon proposed a law permitting a judge to appoint a guardian ad litem for the fetus of every underage woman seeking an abortion, "so that the court may make an informed decision and do substantial justice." With Attorney General Bill Pryor's support, the Alabama House passed the bill in 1999.

Judge Anderson is not alone

Pro-choice advocates across the country can rattle off the names of juvenile judges they advise girls to avoid in almost every county. Judge James Payne in Indianapolis, for example, routinely appointed antiabortion lawyers to represent pregnant girls. Others in Mississippi and Alabama require visits to an antiabortion counseling center before granting a hearing. And in Arkansas, Alabama and Ohio, minors have to travel miles to get to a judge who may actually grant a bypass.

The appeals process offers some relief. When a Florida judge appointed a guardian ad litem for a fetus, the state's highest court overturned his decision. An Indianapolis juvenile judge was similarly overruled. Yet other than the appellate courts, there are few checks on judges operating in closed hearings. Meanwhile, Congress is deliberating a backdoor means of reinforcing "fetal rights" with the Unborn Victims of Violence Act, a bill that would make injuring a fetus—or even a fertilized egg—while committing a federal crime into a new criminal offense. The law would have the effect of defining fetuses at all stages of development as persons, which could potentially jeopardize abortion rights.

The actions of Judge Anderson and others show how far we have fallen since *Roe*, whose central tenet was that before viability, a woman's right to choose always trumps the rights of the fetus. For young women who happen to be in the wrong court at the wrong time, the balance has shifted in the opposite direction, and they may spend a lifetime paying for that bad luck.

10

Abortion Rights Threaten America

First Things

First Things *is a monthly journal published by the Institute on Religion and Public Life, an interreligious, nonpartisan research and education organization whose purpose is to advance a religiously informed public philosophy for the ordering of society.*

The Founding Fathers built the United States on the premise of "ordered liberty," or liberty that stems from a moral truth. "Disordered liberty"—liberty derived from the denial of moral truth—is contrary to the Fathers' vision of America, and it threatens the constitutionally protected human right to life, liberty, and the pursuit of happiness. The most pervasive example of disordered liberty is the power of the courts to establish laws without the consent of the governed, most notably in *Roe v. Wade*, the Supreme Court's 1973 decision that legalized abortion. Americans must work toward reversing *Roe v. Wade* and regaining the power of self-governance.

W e join in giving thanks to Almighty God for what the Founders called this American experiment in ordered liberty. In the Year of Our Lord 1997, the experiment is deeply troubled but it has not failed and, please God, will not fail. As America has been a blessing to our forebears and to us, so will it be a blessing to future generations, if we keep faith with the founding vision.

Invoking "the law of nature and of nature's God," the Founders declared, "We hold these truths to be self-evident." Americans must ask themselves whether they hold them still. We, for our part, answer emphatically in the affirmative. We affirm that before God and the law all are equal, "endowed by their Creator with certain unalienable rights, that among these are life, liberty, and the pursuit of happiness." In recent years it has become increasingly manifest that these truths cannot be taken for granted. Indeed, there is ominous evidence of their rejection in our public life and law.

As leaders of diverse churches and Christian communities, we address our fellow citizens with no partisan political purpose. Our purpose is to help repair a contract too often broken and a covenant too often betrayed. We recall and embrace the wisdom of our first President, who declared in his Farewell Address: "Of all the dispositions and habits which lead to political prosperity, religion and morality are indispensable supports. In vain would that man claim the tribute of patriotism, who should labor to subvert these great pillars of human happiness, these firmest props of the duties of men and citizens." Religion and morality are not an alien intrusion upon our public life but the source and foundation of our pursuit of the common good.

It is in the nature of experiments that they can succeed, and they can fail. President Washington said in his First Inaugural Address: "The preservation of the sacred fire of liberty and the destiny of the republican model of government are justly considered, perhaps, as deeply, as finally, staked on the experiment entrusted to the hands of the American people." We urge the Christians of America to join us in a candid acknowledgment that we have not been as faithful as we ought to that great trust.

Nations are ultimately judged not by their military might or economic wealth but by their fidelity to "the laws of nature and nature's God." In the view of the Founders, just government is self-government. Liberty is not license but is "ordered liberty"—liberty response to moral truth. The great threat to the American experiment today is not from enemies abroad but from disordered liberty. That disorder is increasingly expressed in a denial of the very concept of moral truth. The cynical question of Pontius Pilate, "What is truth?" is today frequently taken to be a mark of sophistication, also in our political discourse and even in the jurisprudence of our courts.

Disordered liberty

The bitter consequences of disordered liberty resulting from the denial of moral truth are by now painfully familiar. Abortion, crime, consumerism, drug abuse, family disintegration, teenage suicide, neglect of the poor, pornography, racial prejudice, ethnic separatism and suspicion—all are rampant in our society. In politics, the public interest is too often sacrificed to private advantage; in economic and foreign policy, the lust for profits overrides concern for the well-being of families at home and the protection of human rights abroad. The powerful forget their obligation to the powerless, and the politics of the common good is abandoned in the interminable contention of special interests. We cannot boast of what we have made of the experiment entrusted to our hands.

While we are all responsible for the state of the nation, and while our ills no doubt have many causes, our attention must be directed to the role of the courts in the disordering of our liberty. Our nation was constituted by agreement that "we the people," through the representative institutions of republican government, would deliberate and decide how we ought to order our life together. In recent years, that agreement has been broken. The Declaration declares that "governments are instituted among men, deriving their just powers from the consent of the governed." In recent years, power has again and again been wielded, notably by the courts, without the consent of the governed.

The most egregious instance of such usurpation of power is the 1973 decision of the Supreme Court in which it claimed to have discovered a "privacy" right to abortion and by which it abolished, in what many constitutional scholars have called an act of raw judicial power, the abortion law of all fifty states. Traditionally in our jurisprudence, the law reflected the moral traditions by which people govern their lives. This decision was a radical departure, arbitrarily uprooting those moral traditions as they had been enacted in law through our representative political process. Our concern is both for the integrity of our constitutional order and for the unborn whom the Court has unjustly excluded from the protection of law.

The great threat to the American experiment today is not from enemies abroad but from disordered liberty.

Our concern is by no means limited to the question of abortion, but the judicially imposed abortion license is at the very core of the disordering of our liberty. The question of abortion is the question of who belongs to the community for which we accept common responsibility. Our goal is unequivocal: Every unborn child protected in law and welcomed in life. We have no illusions that, in a world wounded by sin, that goal will ever be achieved perfectly. Nor do we assume that at present all Americans agree with that goal. Plainly, many do not. We believe, however, that democratic deliberation and decision would result in laws much more protective of the unborn and other vulnerable human lives. We are convinced that the Court was wrong, both morally and legally, to withdraw from a large part of the human community the constitutional guarantee of equal protection and due process of law.

The American people as a whole have not accepted, and we believe they will not accept, the abortion regime imposed by *Roe v. Wade*. In its procedural violation of democratic self-government and in its substantive violation of the "laws of nature and of nature's God," this decision of the Court forfeits any claim to the obedience of conscientious citizens. We are resolved to work relentlessly, through peaceful and constitutional means and for however long it takes, to effectively reverse the abortion license imposed by *Roe v. Wade*. We ask all Americans to join us in that resolve.

Defining liberty

The effort of "we the people" to exercise the right and responsibility of self-government has been made even more difficult by subsequent decisions of the Court. In its stated effort to end the national debate over abortion, the Supreme Court in *Planned Parenthood v. Casey* (1992) transferred the legal ground for the abortion license from the implied right of privacy to an explicit liberty right under the Fourteenth Amendment. The Court there proposed a sweeping redefinition of liberty: "At the heart of liberty is the right to define one's own concept of existence, of meaning, of the universe, and of the mystery of human life." The doctrine declared by the Court would seem to mean that liberty is nothing more nor less than what is chosen by the autonomous, unencumbered self.

This is the very antithesis of the ordered liberty affirmed by the Founders. Liberty in this debased sense is utterly disengaged from the concepts of responsibility and community, and is pitted against the "laws of nature and of nature's God." Such liberty degenerates into license for the oppression of the vulnerable while the government looks the other way, and throws into question the very possibility of the rule of law itself. *Casey* raises the serious question as to whether any law can be enacted in pursuit of the common good, for virtually any law can offend some individuals' definition of selfhood, existence, and the meaning of life. Under the doctrine declared by the Court, it would seem that individual choice can always take precedence over the common good.

Moreover, in *Casey* the Court admonished pro-life dissenters, chastising them for continuing the debate and suggesting that the very legitimacy of the law depends upon the American people obeying the Court's decisions, even though no evidence is offered that those decisions are supported by the Constitution or accepted by a moral consensus of the citizenry. If the Court is inviting us to end the debate over abortion, we, as Christians and free citizens of this republic, respectfully decline the invitation.

The Court has gone still further in what must be described as an apparent course of hostility to democratic self-government. In *Lee v. Weisman* (1992), the Court seemed to suggest that an ethic and morality that "transcend human invention" is what is meant by religion that is constitutionally forbidden ground for law. In *Romer v. Evans* (1996), thousands of years of moral teaching regarding the right ordering of human sexuality was cavalierly dismissed as an irrational "animus." It is exceedingly hard to avoid the conclusion that the Court is declaring that laws or policies informed by religion or religiously based morality are unconstitutional for that reason alone. In this view, religion is simply a bias, and therefore inadmissible in law. Obviously, this was not the belief of those who wrote and ratified our Constitution. Just as obviously, the Court's view is not accepted by the people today. For the Founders and for the overwhelming majority of Americans today, ethics and morality transcend human invention and are typically grounded in religion.

If the Supreme Court and the judiciary it leads do not change course, the awesome consequences are clearly foreseeable. The founding principle of self-government has been thrown into question. Already it seems that people who are motivated by religion or religiously inspired morality are relegated to a category of second-class citizenship. Increasingly, law and public policy will be pitted against the social and moral convictions of the people, with the result that millions of Americans will be alienated from a government that they no longer recognize as their own. We cannot, we must not, let this happen.

Endorsing new rights

Questions of great moral moment for the ordering Q of our life together will continue to demand deliberation and decision. The Court's justification of the abortion license under its debased concept of liberty has brought us to the brink of endorsing new "rights" to doctor-assisted suicide and euthanasia which threaten those at the end of life, the infirm, the handicapped, the unwanted. We are confronted by a radical redefinition of marriage as courts declare marriage to be not a covenanted commitment ordered to the great goods of spousal unity and procreation but a mere contract between autonomous individuals for whatever ends they happen to seek. Under a specious interpretation of the separation of church and state, our public schools are denuded of moral instruction and parents are unjustly burdened in choosing a religious education for their children. These are among the many urgent problems that must be addressed by a free and self-governing people.

Washington spoke of "the experiment entrusted to the hands of the American people." We cannot simply blame the courts for what has gone wrong. We are all responsible. The communications media, the entertainment industry, and educators bear a particular burden of responsibility, as do we Christian leaders and our churches when we fail to instill the hard discipline of ordered liberty in the service of the common good.

A most particular responsibility belongs also to our elected officials in state and national government. Too often, legislators prefer to leave difficult and controverted questions to the courts. This must be called what it is, an abdication of their duty in our representative form of democratic government. Too often, too, Christian legislators separate their convictions from their public actions, thus depriving our politics of their informed moral judgment. The other side of judicial usurpation is legislative dereliction. We must believe that the Constitution bequeathed us by the Founders does not leave us without remedies for our present unhappy circumstance.

Our goal is unequivocal: Every unborn child protected in law and welcomed in life.

The crisis created by *Roe* and its legacy is not without precedent in our national life. Our present circumstance is shadowed by the memory of the infamous Dred Scott decision of 1857. Then the Court, in in a similar act of raw judicial power, excluded slaves of African descent from the community of those possessing rights that others are bound to respect. Abraham Lincoln refused to bow to that decision. It was in devotion to our constitutional order that Lincoln declared in his First Inaugural Address that the people and their representatives had not "practically resigned their government into the hands of that eminent tribunal." Today we are again in desperate need of political leaders who accept the responsibility to lead in restoring government derived from the consent of the governed.

Let no one mistake this statement as an instance of special pleading for Christians or even for religious people more generally. Our purpose is to revitalize a polity in which all the people of "we the people" are full participants. Let no one fear this call for our fellow Christians to more vibrantly exercise their citizenship responsibilities. We reject the idea that ours should be declared a "Christian" nation. We do not seek a sacred public square but a civil public square. We strongly affirm the separation of church and state, which must never be interpreted as the separation of religion from public life. Knowing that the protection of minorities is secure only when such protections are supported by the majority, we urge Christians to renewed opposition to every form of invidious prejudice or discrimination. In the civil public square we must all respectfully engage one another in civil friendship as we deliberate and decide how we ought to order our life together.

Our purpose is to revitalize a polity in which all the people of "we the people" are full participants.

The signers of this statement are by no means agreed on all aspects of law and public policy. We are Catholics, Orthodox, and Protestants of differing convictions on many issues. We are conservatives and progressives of various ethnic and racial identities and with differing political views. We are agreed that we must seek together an America that respects the sanctity of human life, enables the poor to be full participants in our society, strives to overcome racism, and is committed to rebuilding the family. We are agreed that government by the consent of the governed has been thrown into question, and, as a result, our constitutional order is in crisis. We are agreed that—whether the question be protection of the unborn, providing for the poor, restoring the family, or racial justice—we can and must bring law and public policy into greater harmony with the "laws of nature and of nature's God."

Not all Americans are agreed on the implications of those laws, and some doubt that there are such laws. But all can exercise the gift of reason to discern the moral truth that serves the common good. All can attempt to persuade their fellow citizens of the truth that they discern. We Americans are a political community bound to one another in civil argument. Such is the experiment in ordered liberty that has been entrusted to our hands. That experiment is today imperiled, but we are resolved that it continue and flourish, for as it was said two hundred and twenty-one years ago so also it is the case today that "We hold these truths."

11

Threats to Abortion Rights Should Be Challenged

American Civil Liberties Union

The American Civil Liberties Union is a nonprofit organization dedicated to preserving the rights and liberties that are guaranteed by the Constitution and the laws of the United States.

Women fought a long and difficult battle before the right to abortion was won as a result of the 1973 Supreme Court case of *Roe v. Wade*. Legalized abortion improved the lives and health of thousands of women, but anti-choice supporters are enacting laws that make it increasingly difficult for a woman to secure an abortion. Low-income women or women who lack health insurance often find it difficult, if not impossible, to obtain federal funding for an abortion, despite laws that require the government to fund all contraceptive options equally. In most states, young women under the age of eighteen must have their parents' consent to obtain an abortion, unless they convince a judge to waive that requirement. Pro-life advocates challenged the partial-birth abortion procedure, but they failed to achieve presidential approval. Most counties lack an abortion provider, due to the risks posed by violent pro-life activists and demonstrators. America needs to safeguard women's health by challenging these threats to abortion rights.

A woman's decision whether or not to bear a child is one of the most intimate and important decisions she will ever make. Like decisions about contraception, marriage, and child-rearing, the decision to continue or to end a pregnancy is protected from government interference by the U.S. Constitution. Securing full reproductive freedom for all women, regardless of age or economic status, remains among the American Civil Liberties Union (ACLU) highest priorities.

The long march toward reproductive rights

The road to a woman's right to choose has been a long and arduous one. Although abortion was not a crime in this country until the mid-1800s, by the century's end, it was banned in every state. By 1930, an estimated 800,000 illegal abortions were taking place annually, resulting in 8,000–17,000 women's deaths each year. The terrible suffering of tens of thousands of women and their families from botched, back alley abortions moved early reformers like Alan Guttmacher to call for legalization.

A major breakthrough occurred in 1965 when the U.S. Supreme Court struck down a Connecticut law that made it illegal even for married couples to obtain birth control devices. In *Griswold v. Connecticut,* the Court ruled that the ban on contraception violated the constitutional right to "marital privacy." In 1972, the Court extended the right to use contraceptives to all people, married or single. These cases laid the foundation for a constitutional challenge to abortion bans.

Between 1967 and 1971, under mounting pressure from the women's rights movement, 17 states decriminalized abortion. Public opinion also shifted during this period. In 1968, only 15 percent of Americans favored legal abortions; by 1972, 64 percent did. When the Court announced its landmark 1973 ruling legalizing abortion in *Roe v. Wade*, it was marching in step with public opinion.

But the backlash was swift and fierce. Anti-choice forces quickly mobilized, dedicating themselves to reversing *Roe*. In 1974 the ACLU established its Reproductive Freedom Project to advance a broad spectrum of reproductive rights and to resist the anti-choice movement's efforts to undermine women's privacy and equality.

The post-*Roe* struggle

The landmark *Roe v. Wade* decision was based on the constitutional right to privacy—a right the Court found "is broad enough to encompass a woman's decision whether or not to terminate her pregnancy." Characterizing this right as "fundamental" to a woman's "life and future," the Court held that the state could not interfere with the abortion decision unless it had a compelling reason for regulation. A compelling interest in protecting the potential life of the fetus could be asserted only once it became "viable" (usually at the beginning of the last trimester of pregnancy), and even then a woman had to have access to an abortion if it were necessary to preserve her life or health.

The right to choose has dramatically improved the health of individual women by freeing them from the dangers of illegal abortions. It has also improved the quality of women's lives generally, for, as the Supreme Court stated in reaffirming *Roe v. Wade* in 1992, "The ability of women to participate equally in the economic and social life of the Nation has been facilitated by their ability to control their reproductive lives."

The Supreme Court's 1992 decision in *Planned Parenthood v. Casey* was the next legal milestone for reproductive choice. In the face of massive anti-choice pressure, the Court preserved constitutional protection for the right to choose. At the same time however, the Court adopted a new and weaker test for evaluating restrictive abortion laws. Under the "undue burden test," state regulations can survive constitutional review so long as they do not place a "substantial obstacle in the path of a woman seeking an abortion of a nonviable fetus."

The *Casey* decision has forced the ACLU and other pro-choice groups to fight legal battles in courts all over the country over whether or not a particular restriction constitutes a "substantial obstacle." In many cases, the courts have been cruelly insensitive to the problems of real women.

More burdens for low-income women

For decades, opponents of choice have pursued a strategy of imposing special burdens on the most politically powerless women. The Medicaid program, through which the government provides health services to needy people, has long covered all other pregnancy-related services, but the federal government and most states severely restrict Medicaid funding for abortion. As a result, low-income women often find it difficult, if not impossible, to exercise their constitutional right to have safe and legal abortions.

In 1980, the Supreme Court upheld this discriminatory scheme, but in a series of state constitutional cases, advocates for low-income women have successfully argued that when the government provides funding to support the exercise of constitutional rights, it must fund all options evenhandedly, leaving the ultimate choice where it belongs—in the hands of the pregnant woman. These state court victories have made it possible for 40% of Medicaid-eligible women in the U.S. to have access to public funding for abortion.

Women who rely exclusively on the federal government for their health care coverage cannot benefit from state constitutional arguments, however. Through various restrictions on federal appropriations, Congress denies abortion coverage to most federal employees and their dependents, military personnel and their dependents, federal prisoners, Peace Corps volunteers, Native American women, and low-income women who reside in Washington, D.C. Congress has thus created a two-tiered health care system in which women who depend on the government do not have the same rights as those who can afford an abortion or who have private insurance.

Women who depend on the government do not have the same rights as those who can afford an abortion.

In 1991, the Supreme Court upheld regulations forbidding the staffs of federally funded family planning programs from even *mentioning* abortion as a medical option. This "gag rule" on abortion counseling and referral never took effect because former president Bill Clinton rescinded the regulations, but similar gag rules continue to be proposed and have been enforced against organizations that receive U.S. dollars to provide family planning services overseas.

The government has even tried to use its spending power to pressure women *not* to have children. Under the mantle of "welfare reform," state governments are experimenting with policies known as "child exclusions" or "family caps." Aimed at discouraging childbearing by low-income women, child exclusions deny subsistence benefits to children born into families already receiving aid. Because the government has no more business punishing childbearing than restricting abortion, the enforcement of child exclusions violates low-income women's right to choose.

Targeting young women

More than half of the states currently enforce laws that require minors to get permission from their parents or from a court before they can obtain abortions, and many state and local governments continue to deny teenagers the information and services they need to avoid unwanted pregnancies.

Parental involvement laws serve only to deepen the desperation of teenagers already in crisis. While most teenagers who are considering abortion talk to their parents about their decision, some cannot or will not go to their parents no matter what the law says. They fear physical abuse, violence between their parents, being thrown out of the house, or triggering a parent's drug or alcohol problem, among other scenarios. The alternative of going to court for judicial authorization for an abortion is often daunting or futile, and increasing numbers of minors are traveling across state lines for abortions or resorting to dangerous illegal or self-induced procedures.

The states have enacted a web of restrictions that make it more difficult and costly for women to obtain abortions.

The Supreme Court has upheld parental consent and notification laws, but has required that they conform to specific constitutional standards. Careless legislative drafting has led to successful federal challenges. These laws are also beginning to fall under the state constitutions. In 1997, the Supreme Court of California became the third state high court in the nation to hold a parental consent law inconsistent with the state's constitutional privacy protections.

Those who have long sought to make abortion inaccessible to minors are now stepping up their attacks on minors' access to contraception and sexuality education. Proposals to require parental consent for contraceptive services to minors were debated in the 1997 and 1998 Congressional terms and have been cropping up in the state legislatures. If these proposals become law, they will scare many sexually active teenagers away from the family planning clinics that may be their only source of confidential reproductive health care, leaving them vulnerable to higher rates of unintended pregnancy and sexually transmitted diseases including HIV/AIDS.

The proponents of "abstinence-only" sexuality education made gains in 1996 when Congress appropriated $250 million over five years for educational programs that have as their "exclusive purpose, teaching the social, psychological, and health gains to be realized by abstaining from sexual activity." Because such programs must omit any instruction on how to make sex safer, they leave sexually active teenagers unprepared to protect themselves and their partners. While it is important to stress the benefits of abstinence, it is equally important to address the pressing needs of students who reject that lesson.

Banning safe abortion procedures

The latest tactic of the anti-choice movement is to promote so-called "partial-birth abortion" bans. Although these bans are the most widely debated abortion restrictions of the past decade, they are perhaps also the least well understood. The bans' proponents have launched an intensive campaign to portray them as directed against a "single," "late," "gruesome" abortion procedure. The media have adopted and parroted this description. Yet it is wholly inaccurate. Doctors all over the country have testified, and courts all over the country have found, that the language of the bans is broad enough to encompass the safest and most common methods of abortion. Because the bans are thus directed more at abortion in general than at any discrete procedure, they threaten the core right of reproductive choice.

Congress has twice passed, and former president Clinton has twice vetoed, the federal "partial-birth abortion" ban. In his 1996 veto message, Clinton said he could not sign a bill that reflected "Congressional indifference to women's health.". . . Meanwhile, as the debate drones on in Washington, more than two dozen states have enacted copycat bans.

Federal and state constitutional challenges to these state bans are underway throughout the country. In the overwhelming majority of cases, the courts have invalidated the bans. Court after court has identified three main constitutional flaws. First, the language of the bans is so vague that doctors cannot tell with any certainty what conduct is forbidden. Second, the bans lack adequate exceptions to protect women's lives and health. Third, the bans unduly burden the right of reproductive choice by prohibiting the performance of safe and common abortion procedures. These resounding victories in the nation's trial courts are under review in several courts of appeal.

Erosion of access to reproductive health services

Gaining access to reproductive health services has become increasingly difficult. The states have enacted a web of restrictions that make it more difficult and costly for women to obtain abortions. They include requirements for biased counseling that is intended to dissuade women from having abortions; mandatory waiting periods; and excessive, medically unnecessary regulation of abortion providers.

Another barrier to access is the severe shortage of abortion providers. Frightened by anti-choice harassment and violence, many doctors have stopped providing abortions altogether. Eighty-six percent of U.S. counties now have no abortion provider. The shortage is compounded by a persistent lack of adequate abortion training in the nation's medical schools. There are not enough young doctors with both the skills and the courage to step into the void.

Many hospitals have ceased to provide abortion as well. The increasingly frequent mergers between religiously affiliated hospitals and nonsectarian hospitals exacerbate the problem. Such mergers often result in the reduction of reproductive health services because of doctrinal restrictions that the religiously affiliated partner attempts to impose on the new merged entity. Typically, these doctrinal restrictions prohibit hospitals from providing abortion, sterilization, contraceptive services, AIDS prevention services, many types of infertility treatments, and even the "morning-after pill" for rape victims.

In 1989 Justice Harry Blackmun, who wrote the opinion in *Roe v. Wade,* issued a heartfelt dissent from a decision upholding the constitutionality of an array of abortion restrictions. He expressed his fear that, in allowing the government to intrude further and further into the private realm of decisions about reproduction, the Court "casts into darkness the hopes and visions of every woman in this country who had come to believe that the Constitution guaranteed her the right to exercise some control over her unique ability to bear children."

The darkness has not yet descended. But the defense of women's reproductive freedom requires constant vigilance.

12

The Arguments of Abortion Rights Opponents Are Seriously Flawed

Richard North Patterson

Richard North Patterson is the author of numerous legal thrillers, including Protect and Defend, *a fictional novel about late-term abortion and parental-consent laws.*

Research for a fictional novel about abortion uncovered inconsistencies between pro-life arguments and reality. The pro-life lobby argues that late-term abortions result from irresponsible mothers who decide late in their pregnancies that they do not want the child. However, medical experts contend that late-term abortions are rarely performed and usually only in cases of severe fetal abnormalities or when the mother's life is threatened. Pro-life advocates also endorse parental-involvement laws, which are intended to promote family trust. However, a young girl who is afraid of her parents' reaction to her pregnancy is more likely to risk a back-alley abortion than face her parents or a judge. Pro-life laws such as these deny the realities faced by pregnant women.

Two years ago, I set out to research and write a novel of abortion politics focused on the two most vexing issues confronting the pro-choice movement: so-called "partial-birth" abortion and parental consent laws. To do so, I imagined a new federal law, "The Protection of Life Act," which restricted post-viability abortions for minors to cases in which, one, the minor gained the consent of a parent, based on a doctor's advice that the pregnancy posed a "substantial risk" to "life or physical health," or two, a federal court determined that such a risk existed.

My aim was a book, *Protect and Defend*, that was neither pro-choice nor pro-life, but pro-truth, in order to determine whether the understanding of the general public squared with actuality. And what I found was that the politicization of those issues by pro-life forces has created a yawning—and frequently inhumane—gap between reality and myth.

Take so-called "partial-birth" abortion, the subject of such incendiary rhetoric. The majority of the public seems to believe that such procedures are common, that they are a belated means of birth control, performed by callous doctors on the healthy mothers of normal and viable fetuses, and, therefore, that they are a particularly distasteful form of abortion on demand.

The emotional power of this portrait has served the pro-life forces well, allowing them to intimidate politicians while casting pro-choice activists as, at best, oblivious to the moral implications of abortion, even at its most extreme.

The only problem is that none of this is so.

Light years from reality

I interviewed doctors who performed post-viability abortions, women who have had them and a myriad of experts including lawyers, judges, ethicists, activists and mental health professionals. To my regret, the only stakeholders who refused to see me, or to support their argument with fact, were two of the most prominent pro-life groups (though one faxed me grisly diagrams portraying a late-term abortion). I can only speculate as to their reasons. But one thing became very clear: The political version of "partial-birth" abortion is light years from reality.

To start, the term itself is not medical, but invented by the pro-life movement to evoke images of fetuses aborted moments from birth. Yet it is so vaguely defined that many state laws banning "partial-birth" have been struck down by the courts as embracing pre-viability abortions. True late-term abortion is exceedingly uncommon: Only 1 in 1,000 abortions takes place after 24 weeks, out of the total of 1.2 million abortions in the U.S. And because of the risks of harassment or worse, the doctors willing to perform them are about as rare.

Why perform them at all? Not, as we are led to believe, because a prospective mother has tardily concluded that she does not wish to be one. Rather, they result from severe fetal anomalies, a palpable risk to a woman's life or health—or both. Each of the women I interviewed was pregnant with wanted children; none contemplated abortion until faced with pregnancies gone hideously wrong—some of which threatened their own life and health. Yet even though termination was clearly in the interests of both the women and their families, none could relive this experience without lapsing into speechlessness, or even tears. I am aware of no evidence refuting these women as the human face of late-term abortion—certainly the pro-life groups I contacted provided none.

Truth is the first casualty of politics.

But because the procedures required for late-term abortion are not pleasant, the distasteful picture operates to obscure the medical reasons for it. In turn, that has allowed the pro-life movement to vilify a handful of already traumatized women in the service of a larger goal: to erode public support for the right to choose, protected by the U.S. Supreme Court 1973 decision *Roe v. Wade.*

In this case, as happens so often, truth is the first casualty of politics.

Parental consent laws: pointless to dangerous

This maxim also applies to parental consent laws: the requirement of most states that pregnant minors obtain the consent of, or at least notify, one parent before procuring an abortion. The only alternative is for the minor to persuade a court that she is able to make a mature decision, or that abortion is otherwise in her best interests. To many parents, such laws make intuitive sense: We're good parents, we like to believe, and any good parent would want to counsel a daughter at such a moment.

But this Norman Rockwell assumption dissolves on more serious reflection. To begin with, a functional family should not need or require a state or federal law to promote familial closeness. If such a trusting and supportive relationship has not already been established, it is unlikely legislators can create in a moment of crisis what the family has not developed over the course of a child's life.

A functional family should not need or require a state or federal law to promote familial closeness.

And the reasons for such a lack of trust too often involve causes we do not wish to contemplate—ranging from neglect, sexual shame and cultural disdain for women, to insanity, abuse and incest. (One irony, I learned through doctors at urban hospitals, is that incest is a leading cause of the fetal anomalies that lead to late-term abortions.)

Thus the effect of such laws can range from pointless to dangerous. One pregnant girl, afraid to disappoint her loving parents by seeking consent, died from an illegal abortion; another was killed by her own father after disclosing to her mother that he had raped her.

The most common effect of such parental consent and notification laws is that more teen-agers become mothers because they are afraid to ask permission or their parents refuse. In moments of candor, pro-life advocates privately admit that this is a principal aim of such laws, predicting that their passage will lessen the number of abortions.

Teen mothers face a dim economic future

But even were this consequence unintended, it is inevitable: What teen-ager afraid to confront her parents would then have the resources to hire a lawyer or face a judge? And logic dictates that the burdens of teen motherhood will fall on those least equipped for it: the poorest, the least educated, the least resilient. But regardless of demographics, experts tell us that a predictable result of motherhood for any adolescent is depression, economic marginalization and a failure to complete her education.

What, then, are the virtues of such laws? Proponents tell us that parental involvement can spare a minor the psychological trauma of abortion. But experts in adolescent psychology tell us that for most teens an unwanted pregnancy is far more traumatic than abortion and that the best predictor of emotional peace is the ability to decide about it for herself.

An unwilling parent is unlikely to be a good parent; the unwanted children are far more likely to drop out of school or commit acts of violence than children who are wanted, nurtured and well parented. All of these consequences suggest the ultimate failure of such laws: that childbirth compelled by parents, or a fear of parents, leads to familial rupture, not unity.

To me, the clearest lesson is that, in substituting fact for myth, politics debases the serious moral argument that should surround abortion, substituting myth for fact. For the facts impel a conclusion that Americans at large may find surprising: that in the areas of late-term abortion and parental consent, it is the pro-choice forces that can better claim the moral high ground.

Organizations to Contact

The editors have compiled the following list of organizations concerned with the issues debated in this book. The descriptions are derived from materials provided by the organizations. All have publications or information available for interested readers. The list was compiled on the date of publication of the present volume; names, addresses, phone and fax numbers, and e-mail addresses may change. Be aware that many organizations take several weeks or longer to respond to inquiries, so allow as much time as possible.

ACLU Reproductive Freedom Project
125 Broad St., 18th Floor, New York, NY 10004-2400
(212) 549-2500 • fax: (212) 549-2652
website: www.aclu.org

A branch of the American Civil Liberties Union, the project coordinates efforts in litigation, advocacy, and public education to guarantee the constitutional right to reproductive choice. Its mission is to ensure that reproductive decisions will be informed, meaningful, and without hindrance or coercion from the government. The project disseminates fact sheets, pamphlets, and editorial articles and publishes the quarterly newsletter *Reproductive Rights Update.*

Alan Guttmacher Institute
120 Wall St., 21st Floor, New York, NY 10005
(212) 248-1111 • fax: (212) 248-1951
e-mail: info@guttmacher.org • website: www.agi-usa.org

The institute is a reproduction research group that advocates the right to safe and legal abortion. It provides extensive statistical information on abortion and voluntary population control. Publications include the bimonthly journal *Family Planning Perspectives,* which focuses on reproductive health issues; *Preventing Pregnancy, Protecting Health: A New Look at Birth Control in the U.S.;* and the book *Sex and America's Teenagers.*

American Life League (ALL)
PO Box 1350, Stafford, VA 22555
(540) 659-4171 • fax: (540) 659-2586
website: www.all.org

ALL promotes family values and opposes abortion. The organization monitors congressional activities dealing with pro-life issues and provides information on the physical and psychological risks of abortion. It produces educational materials, books, flyers, and programs for pro-family organizations that oppose abortion. Publications include the biweekly newsletter *Communiqué,* the bimonthly magazine *Celebrate Life,* and the weekly newsletter *Lifefax.*

Americans United for Life (AUL)
310 S. Peoria St., Suite 300, Chicago, IL 60604-3534
(312) 492-7234 • fax: (312) 492-7235
e-mail: information@unitedforlife.org • website: www.unitedforlife.org

AUL promotes legislation to make abortion illegal. The organization operates a library and a legal-resource center. It publishes the quarterly newsletter *Lex Vitae,* the monthly newsletters *AUL Insights* and *AUL Forum,* and numerous booklets, including *The Beginning of Human Life* and *Fetal Pain and Abortion: The Medical Evidence.*

Catholics for a Free Choice (CFFC)
1436 U St. NW, Suite 301, Washington, DC 20009
(202) 986-6093 • fax: (202) 332-7995
e-mail: cffc@catholicsforchoice.org • website: www.cath4choice.org

CFFC supports the right to legal abortion and promotes family planning to reduce the incidence of abortion and to increase women's choice in childbearing and child rearing. It publishes the bimonthly newsletter *Conscience,* the booklet *The History of Abortion in the Catholic Church,* and the quarterly *Conscience: A Newsjournal of Prochoice Catholic Opinion,* which serves as a forum for dialogue on ethical questions related to human reproduction.

Center for Bio-Ethical Reform (CBR)
PO Box 3788, Anaheim, CA 92803
(562) 777-9117 • fax: (562) 777-9118
e-mail: cbr@cbrinfo.org • website: www.abortionno.org

CBR opposes legal abortion, focusing its arguments on abortion's moral aspects. Its members frequently address conservative and Christian groups throughout the United States. The center also offers training seminars on fundraising to pro-life volunteers. CBR publishes the monthly newsletter *In-Perspective* and a student training manual for setting up pro-life groups on campuses titled *How to Abortion-Proof Your Campus.* It also produces audiotapes, such as "Is the Bible Silent on Abortion?" and "No More Excuses."

Childbirth by Choice Trust
344 Bloor St. West, Suite 306, Toronto, ON M5S 3A7 Canada
(416) 961-1507
e-mail: info@cbctrust.com • website: www.cbctrust.com

Childbirth by Choice Trust's goal is to educate the public about abortion and reproductive choice. It produces educational materials that aim to provide factual, rational, and straightforward information about fertility control issues. The organization's publications include the booklet *Abortion in Law, History, and Religion* and the pamphlets *Unsure About Your Pregnancy? A Guide to Making the Right Decision* and *Information for Teens About Abortion.*

Human Life Foundation (HLF)
215 Lexington Ave., New York, NY 10016
(212) 685-5210 • fax: (212) 725-9793
e-mail: humanlifereview@mindspring.com
website: www.humanlifereview.com

The foundation serves as a charitable and educational support group for individuals opposed to abortion, euthanasia, and infanticide. HLF offers financial support to organizations that provide women with alternatives to abortion. Its publications include the quarterly *Human Life Review* and books and pamphlets on abortion, bioethics, and family issues.

Human Life International (HLI)
4 Family Lane, Front Royal, VA 22630
(540) 635-7884 • fax: (540) 636-7363
e-mail: hli@hli.org • website: www.hli.org

HLI is a pro-life family education and research organization that believes that the fetus is human from the moment of conception. It offers positive alternatives to what it calls the antilife/antifamily movement. The organization publishes *Confessions of a Prolife Missionary, Deceiving Birth Controllers,* and the monthly newsletters *HLI Reports* and *Special Reports.*

National Abortion and Reproductive Rights Action League (NARAL)
1156 15th St. NW, Suite 700, Washington, DC 20005
(202) 973-3000 • fax: (202) 973-3096
e-mail: comments@naral.org • website: www.naral.org

NARAL works to develop and sustain a pro-choice political constituency in order to maintain the right of all women to legal abortion. The league briefs members of Congress and testifies at hearings on abortion and related issues. It publishes the quarterly *NARAL Newsletter.*

National Conference of Catholic Bishops (NCCB)
3211 Fourth St. NE, Washington, DC 20017-1194
(202) 541-3000 • fax: (202) 541-3322
website: www.nccbuscc.org

The NCCB, which adheres to the Vatican's opposition to abortion, is the American Roman Catholic bishops' organ for unified action. Through its committee on pro-life activities, it advocates a legislative ban on abortion and promotes state restrictions on abortion, such as parental consent/notification laws and strict licensing laws for abortion clinics. Its pro-life publications include the educational kit *Respect Life* and the monthly newsletter *Life Insight.*

National Right to Life Committee (NRLC)
512 10th St. NW, Washington, DC 20004
(202) 626-8800
e-mail: nrlc@nrlc.org • website: www.nrlc.org

NRLC is one of the largest organizations opposing abortion. The committee campaigns against legislation to legalize abortion. It encourages ratification of a constitutional amendment granting embryos and fetuses the same right to life as living persons, and it advocates alternatives to abortion, such as adoption. NRLC publishes the brochure *When Does Life Begin?* and the periodic tabloid *National Right to Life News.*

Operation Rescue National (ORN)
PO Box 740066, Dallas, TX 75374
(972) 494-5316 • fax: (972) 276-9361
e-mail: osa@operationsaveamerica.org
website: www.operationsaveamerica.org

ORN (now Operation Save America) conducts abortion clinic demonstrations in large cities across the country. It pickets abortion clinics, stages clinic blockades, and offers sidewalk counseling in the attempt to persuade women not to have abortions. ORN publishes the quarterly *Operation Rescue National Newsletter* and disseminates a variety of pro-life brochures, pamphlets, and other materials.

Planned Parenthood Federation of America (PPFA)
810 Seventh Ave., New York, NY 10019
(212) 541-7800 • fax: (212) 245-1845
e-mail: communications@ppfa.org • website: www.plannedparenthood.org

PPFA is a national organization that supports people's right to make their own reproductive decisions without governmental interference. It provides contraception, abortion, and family planning services at clinics located throughout the United States. Among its extensive publications are the pamphlets *Abortions: Questions and Answers, Five Ways to Prevent Abortion,* and *Nine Reasons Why Abortions Are Legal.*

Pro-Life Action League
6160 N. Cicero Ave., Suite 600, Chicago, IL 60646
(312) 777-2900 • fax: (312) 777-3061
e-mail: scheidler@attglobal.net • website: www.prolifeaction.org

The league's purpose is to prevent abortions through legal, nonviolent means. It advocates the prohibition of abortion through a constitutional amendment. It conducts demonstrations against abortion clinics and other agencies involved with abortion. The league produces videotapes and publishes various brochures, the book *Closed: 99 Ways to Stop Abortion,* and the quarterly newsletter *Pro-Life Action News.*

Religious Coalition for Reproductive Choice (RCRC)
1025 Vermont Ave. NW, Suite 1130, Washington, DC 20005
(202) 628-7700 • fax: (202) 628-7716
e-mail: info@rcrc.org • website: www.rcrc.org

RCRC consists of more than thirty Christian, Jewish, and other religious groups committed to enabling individuals to make decisions concerning abortion in accordance with their conscience. The organization supports abortion rights, opposes anti-abortion violence, and educates policy makers and the public about the diversity of religious perspectives on abortion. RCRC publishes booklets, an educational essay series, the pamphlets *Abortion and the Holocaust: Twisting the Language* and *Judaism and Abortion,* and the quarterly *Religious Coalition for Reproductive Choice Newsletter.*

Bibliography

Books

Randy Alcorn	*Pro-Life Answers to Pro-Choice Arguments.* Sisters, OR: Multnomah, 2000.
Linda J. Beckman and S. Marie Harvey, eds.	*The New Civil War: The Psychology, Culture, and Politics of Abortion.* Washington, DC: American Psychological Association, 1998.
Mary Boyle	*Rethinking Abortion: Psychology, Gender, Power, and the Law.* New York: Routledge, 1997.
Kimberly J. Cook	*Divided Passions: Public Opinions on Abortion and the Death Penalty.* Boston: Northeastern University Press, 2001.
David J. Garrow	*Liberty and Sexuality: The Right to Privacy and the Making of Roe v. Wade.* Berkeley: University of California Press, 1998.
Faye D. Ginsburg	*Contest Lives: The Abortion Debate in an American Community.* Berkeley: University of California Press, 1998.
Cynthia Gorney	*Articles of Faith: A Frontline History of the Abortion Wars.* New York: Simon and Schuster, 1998.
Mark A. Graber	*Rethinking Abortion: Equal Choice, the Constitution, and Reproductive Politics.* Princeton, NJ: Princeton University Press, 1996.
Mary Guiden	*Partial Birth Abortion.* Denver: National Conference of State Legislatures, 1998.
Kerry N. Jacoby	*Souls, Bodies, Spirits: The Drive to Abolish Abortion Since 1973.* Westport, CT: Praeger, 1998.
Ellie Lee, ed.	*Abortion Law and Politics Today.* New York: St. Martin's, 1998.
Eileen L. McDonagh	*Breaking the Abortion Deadlock: From Choice to Consent.* New York: Oxford University Press, 1996.
Roy M. Mersky and Jill Duffy, eds.	*A Documentary History of the Legal Aspects of Abortion in the United States.* Littleton, CO: Fred B. Rothman, 2000.
Lynn Marie Morgan and Meredith W. Michaels, eds.	*Fetal Subjects, Feminist Positions.* Philadelphia: University of Pennsylvania Press, 1999.
Rachel Roth	*Making Women Pay: The Hidden Costs of Fetal Rights.* Ithaca, NY: Cornell University Press, 1999.

Periodicals

J. Budziszewski   "The Future End of Democracy," *First Things*, March 1999.

Christopher Caldwell   "Why Abortion Is Here to Stay," *New Republic*, April 5, 1999.

Tish Durkin   "Just a Few Questions About Pro-Choice Dogma," *National Journal*, April 7, 2001.

David van Gend   "RU-486: Poisoning the Springs," *Human Life Review*, Spring 2001.

Yvette R. Harris   "Adolescent Abortion," *Society*, July/August 1997.

Barbara Hewson   "Reproductive Autonomy and the Ethics of Abortion," *Journal of Medical Ethics*, October 2001.

Bryan Howard   "Abortion Consent Presents Hazards," *Arizona Republic*, April 23, 1998.

James Kitzpatrick   "A Pro-Life Loss of Nerve?" *First Things*, December 2000.

Judith Levine   "The Dumb-Luck Club," *Index on Censorship*, February 2000.

Judy Mann   "Reduce Abortion and Disarm the Far Right," *Washington Post*, December 1, 2000.

Danielle Ofri   "Common Ground," *Tikkun*, January/February 2002.

Leah Platt   "Making Choice Real," *American Prospect*, September 24, 2001.

Lucia Rayas   "Criminalizing Abortion: A Crime Against Women," *NACLA Report on the Americas*, January/February 1998.

Bob Schaffer   "27 Years of *Roe v. Wade*," *Vital Speeches of the Day*, February 15, 2000.

Elizabeth Schulte   "The New Assault on a Woman's Right to Choose," *International Socialist Review*, June/July 2000.

Annette Tomal   "Parental Involvement Laws, Religion, and Abortion Rates," *Gender Issues*, Fall 2000.

Wendy Wright   "Federal Government Should Not Be in the Business of Funding Abortions," *Insight on the News*, October 29, 2001.

Index